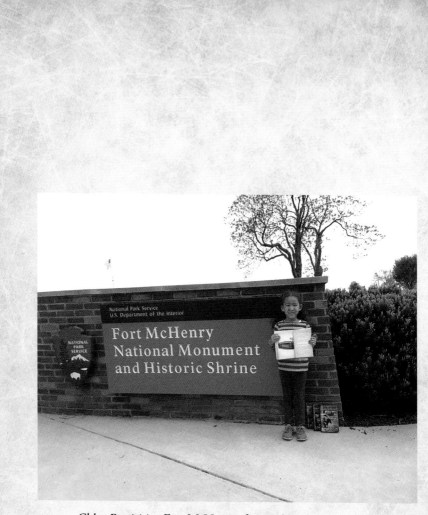

Chloe B., visiting Fort McHenry after reading the book series.
See more at www.RushRevere.com.

Also by Rush Limbaugh

Rush Revere and the Brave Pilgrims
Rush Revere and the First Patriots
Rush Revere and the American Revolution
Rush Revere and the Star-Spangled Banner

Shining the light on history

Rush Revere

and the

PRESIDENCY

Time-Travel Adventures with
Exceptional Americans

RUSH LIMBAUGH

with Kathryn Adams Limbaugh

Historical Writing Consultant: Jonathan Adams Rogers
Children's Writing Consultant: Christopher Schoebinger
Illustrations by Christopher Hiers

THRESHOLD EDITIONS

NEW YORK   LONDON   TORONTO   SYDNEY   NEW DELHI

Threshold Editions
An Imprint of Simon & Schuster, Inc.
1230 Avenue of the Americas
New York, NY 10020

First Threshold Editions hardcover edition November 2016

THRESHOLD EDITIONS and colophon are
trademarks of Simon & Schuster, Inc.

For information about special discounts for bulk purchases,
please contact Simon & Schuster Special Sales at
1-866-506-1949 or business@simonandschuster.com.

The Simon & Schuster Speakers Bureau can bring authors to your live event.
For more information, or to book an event, contact the Simon & Schuster Speakers
Bureau at 1-866-248-3049 or visit our website at www.simonspeakers.com.

Manufactured in the United States of America

9   10   8

Library of Congress Cataloging-in-Publication Data is available.

ISBN 978-1-5011-5689-2
ISBN 978-1-5011-5690-8 (ebook)

This book is dedicated to our beloved nieces and nephews.
You and all young Americans are the future of our country.
Through you, the fundamental values of our nation will live on.

Harmony H., a fan of the book series, with her friend Liberty.

Foreword

*T*he first book in this series, *Rush Revere and the Brave Pilgrims*, was published three years ago. In that time, we have heard from hundreds of thousands of incredible young patriots, like you, from across our great country, who have a newfound love of American history and reading. It is simply heartwarming and wonderful to see. We know that you are our future, and through you, the vision of our country started by amazing Americans like George Washington will be protected.

One of the greatest parts of living in the United States and being an American is the right to vote. In many countries around the world, people do not have this right, and thus cannot participate in government. They have no voice and no say in the decisions being made for them.

The United States of America was founded by exceptional Americans who believed our country should be run by the people, for the people. At the time, this was an entirely new concept. An unelected king or queen who controlled the people and made all decisions ruled most other lands.

The American system of government, including the presidential election process, was an experiment. Amazingly, many of the traditions from the very first presidency are the same today, more than two hundred and forty years later. Others have evolved and developed over time.

Our presidential election process allows Americans to vote for the person they think will be the best leader to carry on the goals and ideals that they personally care about. Every four years, there is an opportunity to vote for a new president or vote to keep the same president in office for a second term.

Leading up to the national election in November, the presidential candidates race around the country, campaigning and getting the word out about why they are running for president. It is our job, as the people, to be fully informed about the candidates and their plans for the country so we can make the best decision.

You may have heard your parents, grandparents, teachers, or friends sitting around the kitchen table, in local diners and restaurants, or across the miles by phone or email talking about their opinions of the candidates. Are they the best leader? Are they saying what I believe in? Do I trust and like them? These conversations can get a little rough sometimes. But because of the importance of what is at stake, they are a fundamental part of being a free American, regardless of whether you agree with the point of view or not.

It is time now to saddle up and *rush, rush, rush* to the next adventure back in time! Get ready to meet some of the most exceptional leaders our country has ever known. . . .

Chapter 1

Sunlight bounced in streaks off the windows of Manchester Middle School as a painter painted the edge of a windowpane. I rode on top of Liberty while he trotted like a proud Spanish stallion through the schoolyard. A gust of wind nearly robbed me of my tricorn hat as a leaf fell from a large oak tree, signaling the end of summer and the start of the new school year.

"Being back at school always feels like coming home," I said to Liberty. "I can't wait to see the time-traveling crew." I dismounted on the sidewalk and happily wiggled my toes inside my tall leather boots.

"I'm sure your students will be excited, too," said Liberty. "I mean, you're practically famous in these parts. You're like the coolest, the most awesome, the most superfun history teacher in the history of, well, history."

I looked at Liberty, suspicious about all of the compliments.

"Um, and on a side note, my stomach is growling, I can hear it. Hello, stomach, yes, I will get you something soon, my little friend. Hey, Revere, how about some snackies?"

I laughed and patted my best friend on his broad brown nose. I knew he was up to something. "Didn't you just have a bucket of oats before we came over?" I asked.

Liberty raised his eyebrows and nodded. His stomach didn't have an off button. Snacks were on his mind 24/7.

Liberty was one of a kind. Even though we'd been friends for some time now, I still marveled at how special he was. A horse who could talk and time-travel—he was truly incredible. When that lightning bolt sent him from the eighteenth century to the twenty-first century, it also gave him a number of extraordinary powers.

"Be sure to stay right here," I urged, pointing to a shady oak tree near the basketball courts. "I shouldn't be long. You remember our good friend Cam, right? His mom texted me saying he had something to ask me and wondered if I would meet him at school today."

"Cam? I love Cam!" Liberty yelled. "He was a member of the time-traveling crew when you were substitute teaching here at Manchester."

"Shh," I said, looking over my shoulder. "Not so loud. You're supposed to be a normal horse, remember? No talking."

"Gotcha, Captain," said Liberty, softly. "On the case. *Normal* is my middle name. Captain Normal, Sir Normal-Lot, King Normal of Normalville."

I just looked at Liberty, and shook my head smiling. "Are you finished?" I asked. Spending time with Liberty was like the arcade game Whac-A-Mole. You never knew when or where his ideas would pop up.

Liberty squinted and nodded distractedly, looking around. "So you say you'll be back shortly, like in ten or fifteen minutes?"

I knew what he was asking. Liberty got bored very easily, so leaving him alone for any period of time was always a risk. I took a deep breath and replied, "Yes, I will return very soon and I need you to be here when I do. And, no, you can't follow me into the school. I know you will be tempted to camouflage yourself and turn invisible to the naked eye, but this time I need you to stay put, understand?"

"Sure thing, *no problemo*, yes, sir!" he replied, standing up straight. Liberty looked convincing, but I wasn't so sure.

"Good, thank you," I said, and started to walk toward the entrance of the school. Then, remembering Liberty's tendency to wander away in search of food, I turned around and said, "And if you are still here when I return, I'll have a treat for you."

"I like the way you think, Revere. What are you waiting for? Chop-chop. The sooner you get back the sooner I eat. Have fun storming the castle. See you soon." Liberty looked up into the tree as if hoping some apples would appear.

I continued walking toward the main entrance. After a few steps, I looked back to see Liberty mouthing a list of possible snacks. "Carrots, apples, peppermints . . . um, did I say carrots?"

Laughing to myself, I walked up the steps and pushed open the double doors. Students hurried past me, bags over their shoulders and books tucked under their arms. "Hey, are you supposed to be Uncle Sam?" asked one of the middle school students. "Or maybe you're Colonel Sanders. Can I get a bucket of chicken?"

"No, that's Benjamin Franklin without the glasses," another replied, laughing.

Rude, I thought. But I guess I couldn't really blame them. It's not every day that a guy dressed in a blue colonial coat, britches, and shiny boots appears at your school. I looked like a model straight out of a colonial magazine.

"Ahoy, good morning!" I exclaimed, smiling widely. I continued to walk down the hallway as the students giggled and jogged away, backpacks slipping from their shoulders. I did not have time to explain that I wore the colonial gear to better teach history to my students.

On the wall was a map of the world that had been tagged with different-colored markers. Flags representing each of the countries were pinned nearby. This was new since my last visit to Manchester Middle. I was so distracted admiring the wall map that I almost collided with Principal Sherman. He seemed to take up the whole hallway.

"Good morning, Mr. Revere, how are you?" Principal Sherman asked, placing two hands on his hips and looking intently at me. "It's good to see you, but I don't think we need a substitute history teacher today."

Principal Sherman wore a long-sleeved button-down shirt, rolled up, with dress pants and shiny black shoes. His hair was neatly cropped and parted formally to one side. His face was fixed in a tough, almost angry expression.

"Good morning, Principal. I am well, thank you. Actually, I am here to see my former student Cam. His mother sent me a text message last night and asked if I could meet him before class."

"Indeed, Mr. Revere, you are always welcome here at Manchester Middle," Principal Sherman said, relaxing his facial expression. He dropped one hand to his side and shuffled a student to class. "I know you are very helpful to Cam when his father is deployed overseas with the military."

"Thank you, sir," I said. He nodded and left, hurrying down the hall and calling after a running student.

My eyes followed Principal Sherman, and I saw framed pictures of teachers and trophies hanging behind glass. A flyer announcing tryouts for the school musical, football game, and upcoming school pep rally were also posted. The chatter and laughter of students could be heard all around.

As I approached the main hallway, I saw one of my former students, Tommy. He had his back to me, but I instantly recognized his blond hair and football jersey. Freedom, another former history student, stood beside him dressed in light blue jeans and a purple sweatshirt. She tapped Tommy on the shoulder and quickly moved to the other side. When Tommy turned to see who had tapped him, she broke out laughing. Tommy smiled.

Finally, I saw Cam walking down the hallway toward the group of students that included Tommy and Freedom. He high-fived everyone in the group. His smile felt contagious. He looked like Tommy's twin, but with a darker complexion and curlier brown hair. He was wearing a T-shirt with a Marine Corps logo and jeans.

It was fun to see the time-traveling crew—Tommy, Freedom, and Cam—together again. When I filled in as the substitute history teacher for Mrs. Borrington, our small crew had some amazing experiences together. Using Liberty's time-travel ability we did so much, including visiting the Pilgrims on the *Mayflower*, walking through the streets of Boston in the 1770s, and joining Paul Revere's Ride. Thinking back on these adventures, I noticed Cam looked happy despite his father being away with the military. So, I was eager to find out what he wanted to ask me about.

Cam nudged Tommy, who picked up a blue backpack off the floor and put his arms through the straps. Tommy nodded to Freedom, and the three friends left the other students and started walking down the hallway. I casually slipped in behind them. I had expected them to notice me, but they just kept walking and talking.

"Did you say president, Cam?" Tommy asked, pausing. "You want to be student body president? Dude, I mean, that is really cool and all, but a ton of work. Aren't you going to be busy enough as the school mascot?"

"Yeah, you're gonna be *awesome* as the Manchester Lion," said Freedom.

"I am pretty excited about it," Cam said. "And I do like the attention. I even had this seventh grader ask for my autograph. So I figured since I'm basically the *Lion King*, I might as well be president, too." He smiled wide and put an arm around each of his friend's shoulders.

Tommy pointed to a poster of Uncle Sam thumbtacked to the wall near a set of lockers. The historical character was pointing straight ahead and below his face were big, bold letters that read I WANT YOU FOR STUDENT BODY PRESIDENT—VISIT

PRINCIPAL'S OFFICE. Tommy chuckled and said, "Sounds like you took Uncle Sam seriously."

"I think 'President Cam' has a nice ring to it, don't you?" Cam said. "If you're lucky, you may be able to live in my White House. I'm just saying." When Cam turned to look at each of his friends I could tell he was grinning from ear to ear.

I was about to surprise the time-traveling crew and make my presence known, when I glimpsed someone coming in our direction. It was a blond-haired girl with a light blue sweater and matching bow in her hair—Elizabeth, the principal's daughter. I ducked and darted into an adjoining hallway and put my back against another set of lockers. A few students looked at me with awkward glances, but I was pretty sure Elizabeth hadn't seen me. She had time-traveled with us the previous school year and tried to change history. Then she attempted to reveal Liberty's secret to her father. Let's just say I wasn't exactly eager to see her.

I peeked around the lockers just as Elizabeth parted the sea of students in front of Cam, Tommy, and Freedom. Three other girls, who looked like her mirror images, followed behind like ducks.

"If it isn't the geek squad," Elizabeth said. "Well, not you, Thomas. Don't forget, I'm saving you a seat right next to me in science class." She gave an eye flutter, then changed to a serious expression as she turned to Cam. "Let me guess, you're planning a nerd convention."

"Actually, Elizabeth," Freedom responded, "Cam is thinking about running for student body president."

"That is the dumbest thing I've ever heard. Can you believe this, girls? I mean, president? Get real."

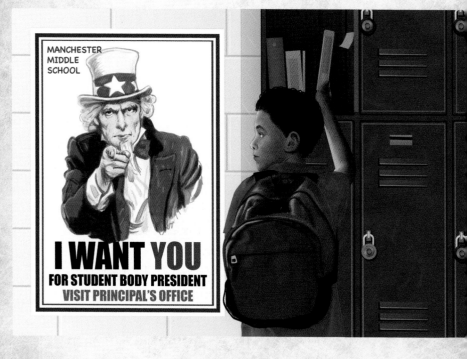

I had not seen Elizabeth in a while and had forgotten how obnoxious she could be.

"Great to see you, too, Eliza-brat," Cam replied.

"Cam, maybe you could be president of Dorks-'R'-Us but no way are you cool enough to be president of Manchester Middle," she said. "Just because you get to wear a stinky lion costume doesn't mean you're outta Loserville."

"Whatever," Cam replied, rolling his eyes.

Elizabeth and her gaggle scurried off, giggling all the way down the hall.

I turned the other way as she passed, then returned to following the crew.

"Do not listen to anything she says," Tommy told Cam.

"Yeah," said Freedom. "Don't let Elizabeth get into your head. Next time she comes around I'm going to throw a bucket of water on her and watch her melt."

"Whoa, Freedom," said Cam. "Maybe I could hire you as part of my presidential security. I need a bodyguard like you."

Freedom smiled and flexed her muscles.

Tommy gave Cam a fist bump. "I gotta go. The bell's going to ring soon, and I still have to get something out of my locker."

"Me, too," Freedom said, and waved goodbye.

Cam was finally alone for a second so I walked over and said brightly, "Hi, Cam!"

"Oh hi, Mr. Revere," Cam responded, happily. "You're lucky. You just missed Elizabeth. I'm telling you she's something else; she totally drives me nuts." He shook his head.

"Oh, no, I'm sorry I missed her," I said, holding back the sarcasm. "So how are you doing? How is your mom?" I asked. "How is your father doing? I'm sure you'll need to get to class soon, but your mom said you wanted to talk to me about something?" Students kept passing in the hallway, looking at my colonial attire with amusement. "Are you okay?"

"That's like twenty questions, Mr. Revere," said Cam, laughing. "So, I was just talking to Tommy and Freedom. The thing is, I want to run for student body president." He pointed at the Uncle Sam poster on the wall. "I mean, I'd be really popular and everyone would have to listen to my ideas. I could make every Friday ice cream day or something. It would be really cool."

"Wow, that is super," I said. "'President Cam.' I like the sound of that."

"Yeah, and I would love to tell Elizabeth and her crew 'No more cheerleading.'"

I raised my eyebrows.

"Okay, I wouldn't really do that, but it's tempting," Cam said.

"This is a great time to be running for school president," I said, "as we have a national presidential election going on right now." My teacher's mind was going full steam.

"Oh yeah," Cam said. "My dad watches all that president stuff. Whenever he calls me he asks who I would vote for if I were old enough. He says when I am eighteen years old, I'll be old enough to vote for the next president of the United States. That will be cool. I get half of what he's talking about and it's pretty interesting and fun, I guess. Anyway, I can't really ask him right now, so that's where you come in, Mr. Revere."

"Thank you for the vote of confidence," I replied, smiling. "I'm with your dad. I watch all of the presidential election stuff, too."

Cam added, "So the only problem is I don't have the first clue about how to run for student body president."

"Well, it's been a long time since I was in middle school, so I don't remember much about student elections myself. I'll need to do some quick studying. But I do know a few things: you need solid ideas, then you need to convince other students to vote for you. And, of course, if you get the most votes, you win. The national election is a little more complicated, but we can talk about that later."

"How hard can that be?" Cam asked. "I mean, I already have great ideas. So it should be pretty easy to get votes and win, right? Piece of cake." He laughed. Cam had a smile that could brighten any room. He almost had me convinced that winning the election would be easy.

I laughed, too, and replied, "Well, I'm not so sure about the piece-of-cake part, but I love the confidence. It is true that having great ideas and getting votes is key. But those are just the first steps in the process. To actually be a leader, whether a president, businessperson, athlete, or any professional, you need to work hard every day, especially *after* you win."

"Oh yeah, sure, after I win, yeah," Cam said, absentmindedly. "President Cam sounds pretty awesome though, right? Hey, when I win, do you think I could get business cards to pass out like on those TV shows? 'Hi, President Cam, nice to meet you.'" He made a motion like he was shaking hands. His eyes were wide and bright. "It would be cool. I would be so popular and kinda famous."

I smiled and said, "Yes, you would get a fancy title like President Cam, but you also get the responsibility that comes with it."

"No problem. I can do it. So easy," Cam said.

I was impressed with Cam's confident attitude but had a feeling running for student body president would be harder than he thought. Candidates running for president planned their election campaigns years in advance. I wondered how much effort it would take in the student elections. Then it struck me.

"For a national election you do certain things before you even begin your campaign," I started to explain. "By the way, a *campaign* is a 'connected series of operations designed to bring about a particular result,' according to the dictionary."

Cam nodded.

I continued, "Under the U.S. Constitution, you need to be a citizen, be at least thirty-five years old, and be a resident of the United States for at least fourteen years. Then you need to file papers with the Federal Election Commission, a government agency that registers candidates."

Cam asked, "What would I need to do to sign up for this election?"

I raised one finger and said, "I have an idea. Since we don't have a lot of time before your class, why don't I reach out to Principal Sherman to set up a meeting for you to ask about the basics—where to sign up, the voting dates, and anything else you need. In the meantime, why don't you think of all of the reasons you want to be student body president and email me. We can take it from there."

His eyes lit up and he said, "Okay, cool, thank you! I'm on it!"

Just then, a bell rang.

"That's my signal, Mr. Revere. Got to run."

"Fantastic," I said. "I'll look for that email and will see you here tomorrow morning."

Cam waved and jogged away, his blue backpack bouncing.

I walked in the other direction, pushed the school doors open to the outside, and walked into the sunlight. I made my way across the schoolyard and, to my surprise, found Liberty actually standing where I left him. In fact, it looked like he was having a conversation with the tree.

"Liberty? What are you doing?" I asked.

He turned and looked surprised to see me. "Oh, hello, Revere."

"Are you talking to that tree?" I asked, quizzically.

"You thought I was talking to a tree?" Liberty asked, letting out a long and hearty neigh. "Who in their right mind would talk to a tree? I was talking to this caterpillar."

I walked closer to the tree and, sure enough, a green caterpillar was clinging to the trunk.

I tried to give Liberty the benefit of the doubt, but this was a bit far-fetched. "A caterpillar?" I asked. "And exactly what were you discussing?"

"I was telling him some of my favorite jokes. So far, he only laughed at one."

I choked back a snicker at the absurdity of what Liberty had just said. "Oh, I see, and which joke did he laugh at?"

Liberty chuckled and said, "What does it mean when you find a horseshoe?"

I shrugged. "I don't know, is it lucky?"

Liberty grinned and said, "Not for me—I'm walking around in my socks!"

I hadn't planned on laughing, but I had to admit the joke was pretty funny. Snickering, I replied, "Nice one, Liberty. And you think the caterpillar enjoyed it?"

"Definitely! It was laughing so hard it almost fell off the tree." Liberty turned his nose until it was inches away from the caterpillar. "Well, bye, little guy. The big boss is back so I gotta go." Then Liberty turned away from the tree as if he talked to caterpillars every day. "So, did you get to see Cam?"

13

"Yes, I did. But first I want to say how grateful I am that you're still here and not, well, you know, horsing around."

"What else would I be doing?" Liberty asked. He looked mildly surprised.

I paused. "Well, you know, like the time you wandered away in Holland, and got stuck in those yellow wooden shoes and knocked into the cheese that rolled into the street? Or the time you kicked off the same shoe through the school window and Principal Sherman blamed Tommy? Or the time you fell asleep and brought Benjamin Franklin back to modern day?"

Liberty looked sheepish. "Okay, okay, you've made your point, Revere. I am pretty good at *horsing around*. But let's not dwell on the past; let's focus on today. So, what did you get me?" Liberty asked wide-eyed. "Wait, wait, let me guess. A giant-sized slice of carrot cake with no frosting? Am I right?"

All of a sudden it hit me. I was so caught up in Cam's excitement, I completely forgot to find the cafeteria and bring Liberty a snack. "Oh no," I mumbled to myself. If Liberty did not eat regularly he could get cranky.

"Um, Liberty, I am afraid I forgot to go to the cafeteria," I said. "I know I promised but I completely forgot. Cam got my mind racing, I'm really sorry." I pulled out a red apple from his saddle-bag and apologetically said, "Here, have this for now. And on our way to Manchester Middle tomorrow morning, we can stop at the bagel shop. Maybe you can even have two bagels. How does that sound?"

Liberty jumped in place and said, "Now we're talking. A double dipper, double trouble . . . you have a deal, Revere. I'm totally there. Spinach bagel, not toasted . . . or wait, maybe an oat bagel . . . oh, so many decisions." Liberty seemed lost in a dream and then woke to say, "Wait, so why are we coming back to Manchester Middle anyway?"

We started walking. "I'm actually helping Cam with an election. He wants to run for student body president."

"Aah," Liberty said. I was pretty sure he was still thinking about bagels.

I explained: "I may have an idea on how we can help Cam. But, of course, it requires your special talents."

"Oooooh, do tell. I mean, what special talents? There are so many for you to choose from," Liberty mused.

I smiled. "Well, I think we may need to use your special time-travel skills."

"Um, you know a horse needs fuel for that kind of travel and use of mental energy. Are there extra bagels in this deal? Actually, maybe extra bagels and maybe an extra slice of carrot cake or two. BOGO—buy one, get one?"

"More than likely, yes. Are you in?" I asked.

Liberty snorted. "Does the American flag have thirteen stripes that represent the original thirteen colonies that represent the thirteen bagels you'll buy for me?"

I raised my eyebrows. "Thirteen? I mean, yes, you're right about the American flag, but thirteen bagels?"

"Time travel isn't cheap, Revere. I mean, if you want to find another horse . . ."

I laughed. Liberty knew he had me cornered. "All right, all right, thirteen bagels it is."

He smiled, contentedly.

We woke up the next morning and visited our favorite bagel shop, Boston Bagels, which was located close to Manchester

Middle School. I grabbed fourteen bagels to go, and we made our way to school to meet Cam. He was standing at the front door as I dropped Liberty off near our favorite oak tree.

"Good morning, Cam," I said as I approached.

Cam looked up. "Hi, Mr. Revere. Did you get my email about running for president?" he asked.

"Sure did—thank you for all the information," I replied. "Great job."

As promised, Cam sent an email the night before listing all his reasons he wanted to become president. I have to admit, I chuckled a bit at some of his thoughts. They included "being cool," "not being told what to do," "having pizza parties," "being popular and famous," and "having everybody love me." Cam wrote nothing about helping his fellow students, doing anything for the school, or being a good leader, so I knew we had work to do. At the end of his email, he wrote in all capital letters,

PRESIDENT CAM, THE COOLEST DUDE AT MANCHESTER MIDDLE.

He didn't quite seem to have the school spirit in mind, just yet.

"What do you think?" Cam asked. "What should I do now?"

I smiled and said, "I brought you a little something that I think will help. Since you want to run for president, every good candidate needs a plan." I pulled out a medium-sized notebook from my workbag. "Here, this is for you. Starting today, you should write down any thoughts or ideas you have about running for president. This will help you as you begin working on your election strategy."

Cam took the notebook and said, raising his eyebrows,

"Thanks, Mr. Revere. Election strategy?" He laughed. "That sounds very professional. I really don't have the first clue about how to start one of those. I was kinda thinking I could just tell my friends I want to be President Cam of Manchester Middle and they vote for me and then I'm president." He shrugged.

I laughed and said, "An election strategy is a series of actions designed to get you a particular result. It is like a team game plan. Every good coach has a playbook, so that is your election playbook."

"Got it," said Cam, energetically. He smiled and picked up his new notebook. "So I'm trying to get the most votes, right?"

"Absolutely, you are trying to get the *majority* of votes to win, but there is a lot to do before then."

"Cool," said Cam. "What do I do first?"

"I thought about this a lot last night," I replied. "So, you know how Tommy studies great quarterbacks to learn how to throw good passes? Well, I'm thinking we should study some of the best leaders in our history to learn how to win this election. We could enlist Liberty and go back in time to learn from the best."

"Sounds awesome, but how do we do that? I mean, who would we visit?"

"Here's what I'm thinking. I called Principal Sherman and asked if I could organize an after-school club. He said yes, as long as we have at least ten students and their parents approve. He also said we can use one of the classrooms after school is out."

"Okay, awesome," Cam said. "So, who will we go see first?"

I smiled widely, thrilled with Cam's excitement, and said, "Who would be better than the first president of the United

States? You want to be student body president, right? I can't think of a better person to learn from first than George Washington."

"Oh, good one. Okay, I'm in." Cam said.

"If you remember, the last time we saw George Washington was in 1776, but he wasn't president yet. At that time, he was leading America's Continental Army against the mighty British superpower."

"Oh yeah, I remember that," Cam said. "He wanted to recruit Liberty to be one of his soldiers, but Liberty passed out at the thought of it." We both laughed at the recollection.

"There was so much going on with the war and everything, but George Washington was really awesome and nice to me," said Cam.

I nodded. "When we go back in time to see George Washington this time, he will be president. I hope he will have some tips for you about how to run your campaign. And more importantly, how to *be* a good president, if you win."

"Awesome," Cam said, pumping his fist. "I knew you were the best person to ask, Mr. Revere."

"Well, thank you very much. It is an honor to help, and I know your dad will be proud to hear about your plan to run for office," I said.

"But, wait, who's going to be in the club?" Cam asked. "What are we going to do?"

"You should invite Tommy and Freedom, of course. But we'll need to recruit at least seven more. I'm sure you'll want Elizabeth in the club, right?" I winked.

Cam laughed. "Good one, Mr. Revere. But I'd rather play soccer with a hive of angry bees."

I was glad that Cam wanted to avoid Elizabeth. But I had a feeling the two of them were on a collision course—just like the American Patriots and King George III.

That afternoon, around fifteen minutes before the start of classes, Cam and I arrived at Principal Sherman's office. We said hello to the school administrator, and she asked us to take a seat. After a few minutes, Principal Sherman opened his door. He seemed to take up the whole doorway, and he wore a serious expression.

"Mr. Revere and Cameron, good afternoon. Come on in," Principal Sherman said. He held out his hand to guide us, and we entered his office and sat down in the two leather chairs facing his desk.

"Thank you very much for seeing us, Principal. Cam had a few questions about the upcoming student body elections," I said.

Cam nodded nervously, sitting up straight in his chair. He looked at the picture of the principal's family, including Elizabeth Sherman. "Yes, Principal Sherman, um, I want to run for president, but I don't really know what to do, so Mr. Revere said to come get the rules."

Principal Sherman did not smile as he pulled a stapled packet of paper from his desk drawer. He handed the document to Cam. "Here you go," he said seriously. "Read through this packet for all the details about the election. Your first step is to fill out the candidate application. You should fill out all the reasons you want to be student body president."

"Okay," Cam said quietly, looking at the typed text.

Principal Sherman leaned forward in his chair. "In a little over a month every student at Manchester Middle School will vote for anyone who is running for each position. Simply, the student with the most votes is elected."

"Easy enough," Cam said, flipping through the pages.

"Not so fast," Principal Sherman said, looking intently at Cam. "The rules in that packet must be followed *exactly*, or else the candidate will be disqualified. There are limits on the number of posters, how much you spend, what you give away, your use of social media, and on your conduct during the election. If the teachers supervising the election find that any of the rules are broken, you will not be elected."

"That is very important to remember," I said softly to Cam. "Make sure to read that packet a few times to get all the rules."

"Excellent," Principal Sherman said, as he rose. We understood that it was time to leave and got up to go. "The big event to add to your calendar is the candidates' speeches the day before the election. There, you will get to tell the other students about yourself and what you plan to do for your school."

"Sounds good. Thank you, Principal Sherman," Cam said as we walked out of the office.

Chapter 2

*O*ver the next days, I worked on the details of our new club. Instead of holding open sign-ups for the whole school, I decided it made the most sense for the time-traveling crew—Tommy, Freedom, and Cam—to recruit seven other students who loved to explore, liked current events, and wanted to join the club. We held our first meeting a week later, after school.

"Great to see everyone!" I exclaimed, as I walked through the classroom door.

"Hey, Mr. Revere!" Tommy called out. His intelligent blue eyes and wide smile followed me as I made my way to the teacher's desk at the front of the room. "Where's Liberty?"

"Hello, Tommy, it's great to see you, again." I said. "Liberty is outside, I hope."

"Good afternoon, Mr. Revere," Freedom said sweetly. A ribbon in her long, straight black hair caught my attention.

It was bright red, white, and blue. The patriotic colors made my heart tap a beat.

"I really like your ribbon, Freedom," I said, smiling.

"Thank you, my grandpa gave it to me for my birthday," she replied. "I don't know if it really matches my shirt, but that's okay."

"I was totally going to wear the same ribbon, but I forgot it in my locker. My bad. We could have been twinsies," Cam teased. He took off his blue baseball cap and pretended to clip a ribbon in his hair.

Freedom skeptically looked over at Cam with her thoughtful brown eyes. She shyly said, "Thank you, Mr. Revere and Cam . . . I think."

Other students filled in the seats behind and around the time-traveling crew. It was fun to be in front of a class again.

I began the club meeting by saying, "Welcome, everyone, to our first club meeting. My name is Mr. Revere and I am thrilled to be your club leader and teacher. No applause necessary."

I jokingly raised my hand as if to silence the roaring crowd at a concert. Realizing that the students were staring at me blankly, I decided to save comedy for another day. I continued, "I know all of you have been working hard in school all day, so I want to assure you that we will play a lot of games in this club. We will discuss what is happening in our country today and have some fun with history."

I was interrupted by a knock at the door. *This is unexpected*, I thought. All ten students were sitting right in front of me.

"Come in," I said.

The door opened and a pizza delivery guy walked in wearing a bright red shirt and cap. "I have your three pizzas," he said.

"Um, I didn't order any pizzas," I replied.

Tommy sighed with delight. "Oh, man, those pizzas smell delicious."

"The receipt says they were paid for by a Mr. Liberty," said the pizza guy.

I rolled my eyes.

Cam cheered. "That's my boy, Liberty!" He jumped out of his seat and happily took the pizza boxes. He brought them over to three empty desks as the other students crowded around, each taking a slice.

"One of these is a vegetarian pizza," said Freedom. "I bet I know who wants a piece of this one."

Just then, a flash of brown popped up and down in the open window on the side of the room. "Liberty!" I gasped. Liberty's long nose appeared in the open window and he let out a whinny. *So much for keeping a low profile out by the tree,* I thought.

Freedom ran over to the window, carrying a slice of veggie pizza. "Hi, Liberty," she said, feeding him some vegetables from the top of the slice. The students unfamiliar with Liberty gawked at the sight of real horse sticking its head through the classroom window. Within seconds, everyone walked over to pet him.

A young boy with a mouth full of pepperoni and cheese looked at me and said, "Mr. Revere, there's a horse in our window." I nodded, not exactly sure how to respond.

"This is the best club, ever!" said another boy. "Pizzas . . . horses . . . what's next?"

I wasn't sure how or when Liberty ordered pizza. I just smiled, grabbed a slice, and made the obvious introduction. "This is Mr. Liberty, better known as Liberty. He's my traveling companion. His two favorite things are food and history. Sometimes I use his name when I order pizzas. I guess I forgot that I had done that." I smiled awkwardly, and then gave Liberty a dirty look.

Liberty looked pleased with himself, soaking up all the attention.

"Now then, let's continue while we eat," I said. "Does everyone know that we are in the middle of a national presidential election campaign?"

Most members of the club nodded.

"Excellent, so on the first Tuesday after the first Monday in November, Americans vote for the candidate they think is the best to lead the country."

Cam jumped in and said, "There's an election going on right here at Manchester Middle, too. Just saying."

Tommy laughed. "Wow, man, really? I didn't know that. Oh wait, I wouldn't except for the other one hundred times you've said it."

The class laughed.

"Right, Cam. Along with the national election, Manchester Middle School also will be having an election. Pretty cool, isn't it?"

The class seemed to shrug in unison as they ate pizza.

"But before we look at today's current events, we need to work out some basics for the club. I think that every great club needs an equally great name. What do you guys think? Does anyone have a club name idea?"

"I have one. How about the *Eagle Spies?*" said Tommy.

Cam coughed as if he was clearing his throat and said, "Lame," under his breath.

Tommy looked over at Cam and mouthed, "What-ev-er, dude."

"How about *Young Travelers?*" Freedom suggested.

Cam made the same exaggerated coughing sound and said, "Double lame," just loud enough for everyone to hear.

"Well, I don't see you coming up with a genius answer," Freedom responded, giving Cam a playful shove.

Liberty popped up and down like a jack-in-the-box in the window. The students turned and laughed.

I'm sure he was desperate to say something. Knowing Liberty, he would probably play a game of charades. And who knows where that would lead. Before he could, I said, "I have an idea: how about we break up into a mini-Congress session, so you can think as teams? What can I say—I am an American history teacher, after all."

"Sounds good to me," Cam said.

The other students nodded, looking unsure. They broke into groups of two and over the next fifteen minutes brainstormed name ideas.

I took the opportunity to walk over to the window and see what Liberty was up to. I whispered, "I assume you have something to say? Make sure you whisper so the whole class doesn't hear you."

Liberty barely moved his lips and said, "I have a club name idea. How about the *American Adventurers?*"

"Hmm, *American Adventurers,*" I repeated, softly. I liked the way it rolled off my tongue. "But, why Adventurers?"

Liberty looked at me as though I was missing some brain cells. "Duh, because I think adventures are fun, and I want to time-travel and see lots of fun things. And because we are American and you teach American history. I put the two words together and, voilà."

I took a quick breath and said, "Liberty, I think you may be on to something."

"Coming through for you is what I do," beamed Liberty. "I'm the peanut butter to your jelly. I'm the frosting to your cake. I'm the cheese to your pizza."

"Speaking of pizza," I accused.

"You don't have to thank me," said Liberty. "I just wanted to make you look good. You know, with this being the first club meeting and all."

"Aha," I replied, not really knowing what else to say. I had planned on scolding Liberty for ordering pizza without consulting with me. Finally, I said, "Well, that was very thoughtful of you. But how did you order it?"

Liberty shrugged, "Your phone is easy to navigate with my lips."

I cringed at the thought of Liberty's mouth all over my phone.

I leaned my head back and closed my eyes, shaking my head. "So, I suppose you are going to hang out right here in the window instead of over by the tree like we planned?"

Liberty grinned. "Revere, don't worry about little old me at all. I'll be right here minding my own business. You can just call me your silent observer, your partner in crime. You know, like a window curtain blowing in the breeze but quietly."

I just shook my head and smiled.

After a few minutes, a representative from each group presented a name to the class.

Cam stood up and said, "The best name our group came up with is *Captain America*. Cool, right?"

Cam sat down and Tommy stood and said, "Our group came

up with *History Hunters*. But I personally like . . ." He cupped his hands around his mouth and called out, "Huh, Huh, Hullabaloo History Crew!" Tommy bowed and smiled. "Thank you, thank you. I'm here all week."

When the class clown sat down, Freedom stood and calmly said, "We chose the *American Adventurers*." She turned and winked at Liberty.

I had forgotten that Freedom and Liberty had a special connection. Freedom's unique love for animals and Liberty's special gifts allowed them to read each other's minds.

Once they were finished I said, "In honor of the presidential election season and because the right to vote is an important part of our history, each of you gets to vote for the name you like the most. Let's start with *American Adventurers*. All in favor, raise your hand," I said.

All hands rose high into the air. There was a loud tapping on the windowsill as Liberty tried to raise his one hoof. So much for silent observer. The whole class started to laugh.

"Oh, wow, it's unanimous. Do you know, this is exactly what happened when George Washington was elected to be the first president of the United States in 1789," I said. "It was the only time in American history that a president was elected by all voters." I paused to let that sink in, and then added, "Well, that makes it easy. You all are in agreement, we are now officially the *American Adventurers*."

While the other students were happily chatting with each other, Cam walked up to me and privately said, "So, Mr. Revere, if getting votes for my president's race is that easy, I'll have it in the bag, no problem."

"Yes, it would be, I suppose, but George Washington's

unanimous victory was the first and last time it happened in American history. In every presidential race since then, the votes have been split almost equally between different candidates. Getting votes is a lot harder than it seems. Oh, and I haven't even started on how hard it is to lead and serve others once you win."

"Gee, thanks for the pep talk, Mr. Revere," Cam said with a shrug. His shoulders slumped a bit under his bright yellow T-shirt.

"I'm sorry, Cam. Actually, elections are really exciting. Just like when you play a tough basketball opponent, your game often rises to meet the challenge."

Cam looked at me skeptically.

"It's true. But rather than learn this from me, let's hear it from some of the greatest leaders in history. How about we go and try to speak with George Washington about his time as president. I bet you will pick up some great tips on both running for office and also leading. That should fill up your playbook pretty quickly."

"Awesome, let's get Liberty and go," Cam offered. "I'm pumped to go back in time again."

Seven of the club students had never time-traveled or had a clue about Liberty's ability to talk. I knew we couldn't take the entire group with us to the eighteenth century, so I whispered to Cam to meet me out by the large oak tree right after our American Adventurers club wrapped up for the day. I was about to walk over and tell Liberty the plan when I realized he was no longer in the window. *Where is Liberty now?* I thought to myself. I hoped he was planning to meet me back at the tree.

After all the students left the room, I headed out to meet Cam by the oak tree. I walked down the hallway, fully content with the day and minding my own business. Out of nowhere, Elizabeth came bouncing along next to me.

"Mr. Revere, what are *you* doing here?" she asked, suspiciously. She flipped her blond hair and placed a hand on her hip, blocking my path. She looked like a miniature version of her father, Principal Sherman.

Startled, I replied, "Elizabeth, so wonderful to see you. I just finished a great club meeting and was heading out for the day."

"What club meeting?" she asked with piercing eyes trained on mine.

I felt some hesitation but said with pride, "It is an after-school club and we are called the American Adventurers."

"And I wasn't invited," Elizabeth said. Then under her breath, "I know what you're up to."

"I'm sorry, what was that?" I said, leaning toward the exit.

"I said I haven't forgotten about your silly talking horse or *the crew,* as you call them, jumping back in time."

I took a deep breath, remembering the time when Elizabeth followed us back in time to England in 1765 and tried to side with King George against the Americans.

Smiling goodbye, I sidestepped past her in the hallway and picked up my pace to meet up with Liberty and Cam.

"Did you take a nap on your way here?" Liberty asked, laughing to himself. He was standing in the shade, with Cam leaning on his saddle in a casual way.

"Sorry, Liberty. I was briefly delayed by your favorite friend, Elizabeth."

Cam rolled his eyes. "Oh great. She's always around when you don't want to see her."

Liberty gasped and shook a little at the thought of Elizabeth.

"Does she know we're planning to time-travel to visit George Washington?" Cam asked.

I shook my head and replied, "No, but let's hurry so she doesn't see us out here and grow suspicious."

"Mr. Revere, I can't time-jump wearing these clothes. I won't fit in," said Cam.

"No worries, I've got you covered." I pulled out a set of colonial clothes from Liberty's saddlebag.

Cam put his tan breeches and a colonial white shirt on over his school clothes. He switched his sneakers to black formal shoes.

"Don't forget your playbook," I said.

"Got it right here." He tapped on the side of Liberty's saddlebag.

"Perfect, okay. So, Liberty, we need to find George Washington, New York, April 30, 1789, Inauguration Day," I said.

"Gotcha, Captain," He pretended to program a miniature computer.

"Ready, Cam?" I asked.

When Cam and I jumped up onto Liberty's saddle, Liberty exclaimed, "*Rush, rush, rushing to history!*"

The swirling yellow and purple circular time portal opened and Liberty jumped into the fog. After a few dizzying spins, we passed through to 1789. Liberty's hooves hit the dirt road running.

"Hey, that was a pretty good landing, wasn't it?" Liberty asked, looking up at us with a smile. "If we were on a plane, I'm pretty sure the passengers would be clapping."

Cam and I clapped, looking at each other with eyebrows raised.

As we moved up the street we saw crowds gathering like before a baseball game. Everyone seemed like they were in a party mood, with banners hanging from windows. All were talking loudly.

A man pushed past us hustling down the street. "God bless His Excellency George Washington the Great!" he yelled, drawing appreciative claps from others lining the roads.

I looked around as people pushed past and said, "Let's find a quiet corner and figure out where we are." Cam and I dismounted from Liberty, and I searched my jacket pocket for my 1789 map of New York City.

"Knock, knock," said Liberty.

"Who's there?" answered Cam.

"Noah."

"Noah who?"

"Noah a good place to eat around here?" Liberty smiled and wiggled his eyebrows.

"Good one, Liberty," said Cam. "But we just ate pizza."

"And you had a bucket of oats right before that," I added.

"I didn't say I needed a snackie snack right now," Liberty explained. "But it's good to be prepared. You know, when we're all famished we'll want to know the fastest way to get food."

Finding a quiet spot and ignoring Liberty, I pulled out the map and studied the streets for a few moments. I said, "Okay, guys, I see where we are in New York now. It shouldn't be that difficult to find our destination. Let's take a second to remember where we are in American history and what led us to this point in time. Cam, do you remember when Tommy told you about meeting William Bradford—the leader of the Pilgrims?"

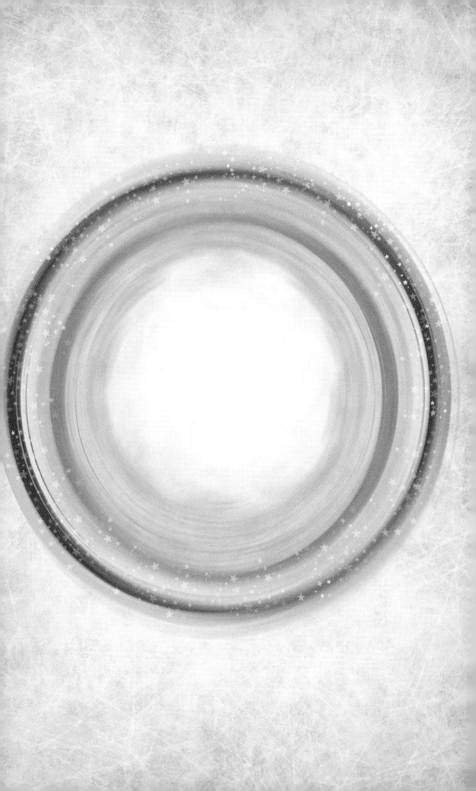

"Um, yeah, I think so. I wasn't at Manchester Middle yet but I remember Tommy telling me when you guys landed on the *Mayflower* boat and he almost fell overboard," Cam replied.

"Exactly right," I said. "Great memory. One of our first time-travel adventures was to the deck of the *Mayflower* in 1620 when the Pilgrims were crossing the ocean to what we now know as North America."

Liberty started to giggle. "Did Tommy tell you about the poop deck?"

I smiled and shook my head at Liberty's antics. I continued, "After the Pilgrims survived the incredibly difficult sixty-six-day journey across the rough Atlantic waters to the New World, they began to develop their towns and eventually colonies and states. Remember, the Pilgrims were in search of religious freedom when they came to the New World, and that is why they left England and the King's rule."

Cam nodded, paying close attention.

"The odds were against the Pilgrims," I went on. "There were no Home Depots or grocery stores stocked with food for them when they arrived. They struggled through harsh winters and, amazingly, they not only survived but thrived."

Liberty shook his body as if he was about to deliver his best joke. He added, "Oh, and after the Pilgrims arrived in the New World they grew the most amazing corn. They corn-ered the market on corn. Get it?"

I tried to hold a straight face. "Well, technically their Native American friend, Squanto, taught them how to grow corn. Remember Squanto showed Freedom how to plant each corn seed with dead fish?" I said.

"Really? A fish?" Cam asked.

I nodded. "As the colonies formed, the early Americans realized they could be independent and didn't have to be under the rule of the King. Eventually, the colonists became a ragtag group of American Patriots fighting against unfair taxes, led by America's Founding Fathers."

Liberty nodded and added, "Yahhh, totally true, Revere. The Americans declared independence on July 4, 1776, but had to keep fighting the mean old British for a long time. They were totally outnumbered and outfunded . . . and there were a lot more *outs*."

Liberty continued excitedly, "It was like your dodgeball game against Billy the Bully, right, Cam?"

Cam laughed. "Oh yeah, totally! Billy the Bulldozer more like. That guy is massive," Cam said.

"No question," I said. "But just like you in your dodgeball game, as you know the Patriots fought hard and eventually won their freedom."

Cam asked, "So how did George Washington become president? I mean, I'm guessing there weren't any posters hanging around on walls like at Manchester Middle."

Liberty and I laughed. "Basically, the early American Patriots realized that, along with the Congress and the Supreme Court, they needed a president to be the face of the nation; otherwise there would be no real leader. But they also knew they did not want to go back to the rule of a king. Remember that King George III was not elected. The Americans fought the Revolution to fight against this rule, so it was hard for them to figure out who would lead. Still, they knew someone had to be in that position, but elected, and there to serve the people. Have you ever been in a situation where everyone has a lot of ideas but no one makes a decision? A president is there to make them."

Liberty and Cam nodded. A passing carriage kicked up dust that formed a cloud around us.

"Flash-forward to today, April 30, 1789, one hundred and sixty-nine years after the Pilgrims landed on Cape Cod. Our first president, George Washington, is about to be inaugurated, right here in New York City."

The crowd around us was getting larger and more boisterous. I pointed to the map and said, "We need to head down this street and all the way down to Federal Hall on Wall Street."

"Wall Street, you mean like where they trade stocks?" Cam asked, looking up at me innocently. "My dad watches those money shows whenever he's home and he always tells me to pay attention to the stock market. I don't really know what he means, but I watch anyway." He laughed.

"We will save stocks for another day, but you are exactly right, Cam. Yes, on April 30, 1789, Federal Hall was the home to Congress. In the month right before this, the House and Senate have been working out how the inauguration will be conducted," I said.

A girl with a banner skipped down the street beside us.

I pulled out a crisp carrot from Liberty's saddlebag and offered it to him.

"Thank you," he replied. Munching, he said, unfazed, "By the way, isn't that George Washington?" He pointed with his nose.

The crowd around us seemed to surge forward.

"Whoa, it is him," Cam said. "He looks a little older than when we saw him before but that's totally the guy. He's taller than everybody else. Do you see him?"

Sure enough, it was George Washington walking ahead of us.

"Let's go, guys, we don't want to miss this," I said.

"How are we going to talk to George Washington with all these people?" Cam asked.

Washington was surrounded by a sea of people pushing him forward. In the chaos, he was swarmed like a modern celebrity at a big event. He was elegant and graceful and did not seem to be in a rush, gliding through the crowd as they pushed and nearly elbowed him.

"Where is the Secret Service?" Liberty asked. "You know, the people with dark glasses and radios in their ears who walk around and protect the President?"

I replied, "There was no Secret Service in 1789, Liberty. In fact, it was not created until nearly one hundred years later, in 1865, during the Civil War. Here is a little bit of fun trivia for your next dinner party: at first the Secret Service's job was to find counterfeit money. Now they protect the President."

Cam nodded. "That's awesome. I like finding money."

"I like finding vegetable gardens," said Liberty, nodding.

A man pushed through the crowd and placed his hand on Liberty's saddle for support.

"Hey, buddy," Liberty yelled, "back away from the saddlebag. My snacks are in there!"

The man looked shocked, backed up, and fell over into a tub beside the road. Water splashed over a woman dressed in fine clothes, who yelled at the man. Wet in the tub, the man pointed at Liberty, who looked just like any horse on the street. The drenched woman eyed the man with disgust and walked away.

I turned to see Cam doubled over, laughing.

Shaking my head, I said, "We'd better get going. We are losing George Washington."

We pushed further into the crowd that was growing larger as we neared Federal Hall. Men carried children on their shoulders. The crowd was a sea of red, white, and blue. Flags were flying and banners were raised. As we turned a corner the noise of the crowd became intense. Everyone seemed to be talking at once and pointing to a building in the middle of the square.

"I think you lost him, Revere," Liberty said, shaking his hindquarters to move people gently out of the way.

"No, I didn't," I said.

Cam and Liberty both paused and looked at me expectantly.

"So where is he?" Cam asked.

"From the history I read, he should be in Federal Hall's Senate Chamber right now. In a few minutes, he and Vice President John Adams will walk onto that balcony, right there." I pointed.

We all looked up. Federal Hall was topped with a large spire, like on a church bell tower, and below it a triangular facade like the modern U.S. Capitol Building, then pillars. On a bronze fence at the front of the balcony, flags were draped.

"Can we get any closer?" Cam asked. "I can barely see anything."

"Aye, aye, young crew member. I hear you loud and clear," Liberty said. He pushed his way through the crowd toward the center, about fifteen feet below the balcony.

"Pretty good seats, Liberty," I whispered, as Cam climbed up onto his saddle. Everyone around us seemed so happy they didn't even notice us. We all looked up to the empty balcony.

All of a sudden the crowd roared. A woman shouted, "God bless General George Washington!" and waved her scarf.

"Long live George Washington!" yelled another.

"Long live the United States of America!" exclaimed a third.

A group of men led by George Washington emerged onto the balcony of Federal Hall.

"Those guys don't look like the Secret Service, either, right?" Cam said, brown eyes focused on the well-dressed men above.

I replied, "Right. Those are the senators and representatives. Remember when we learned about Congress on our field trip to Washington, D.C.?"

Cam nodded.

George Washington bowed to each congressman as he passed. I pointed ahead and said, "That man there is the highest-ranking judge in New York State, Robert Livingston. He will soon be administering the Presidential Oath to George Washington."

"Presidential oats?" asked Liberty. "As in a bucket of oats for the President? Wow, it really pays to be president."

"Not oats," I clarified. "'Oath' with the letter *h* at the end. The Presidential Oath is one of the traditions of the American presidency. It is what someone must promise before becoming president."

Cam perked up. "I didn't know you made promises when becoming president. I wonder if I need an oath when I win."

"The Presidential Oath is included in the Constitution. Everyone, from George Washington to our current president, has said the same oath, for hundreds of years. When our next president is elected every four years in November, he or she will repeat the same oath that every president has said before, in January of the following year."

"That's really cool," Cam said, eyes focused on Washington.

President George Washington placed his hand on what I knew was a Bible and began to speak.

"See if you can hear the words. George Washington is the first person ever to speak these words to become president," I said.

We listened closely. George Washington's words were faint over the crowd, who quickly became silent as everyone strained to hear.

"I do solemnly swear," he said, "that I will faithfully execute the office of President of the United States . . ."

"I can barely hear him," whispered Liberty, leaning in.

". . . and will to the best of my ability, preserve, protect, and defend the Constitution of the United States."

"That's awesome," Cam said.

"Listen, listen," I said calmly. "This is really important."

George Washington added, "So help me God," in a soft scratchy voice. Then he leaned in and kissed the large Bible in Robert Livingston's hands.

The crowd erupted and the sound in the square pounded in my ears.

"WASH-ING-TON, WASH-ING-TON," Cam began to chant, raising his arms to entice the other members of the crowd. One looked at him sideways and instead yelled, "Three cheers for President George Washington!"

The crowd yelled in unison, "Hip-hip-hooray, hip-hip-hooray, hip-hip-hooray!" and everyone on the balcony bowed to the first President of the United States, George Washington. I heard the firing of thirteen canons. They sounded like loud, deep fireworks one after the other.

Then George Washington came to the edge of the balcony and looked out toward us.

I could see the lines on his face, his powdered hair, and his brown coat. I was close enough to see the metal buttons on his jacket. He also wore white stockings and a sword at his waist.

Washington bowed and the crowd cheered again.

Someone shouted, "Long live President George Washington!" He then turned and walked through the door back to the Senate Chamber. Behind him followed the members of Congress. We stayed and stared at the empty balcony. I was in awe.

"That was truly incredible," I said.

"Yeah, I think I need to learn to bow like that. The crowd really loved it," Cam said, trying to do an impression of George Washington's bow.

I smiled and said, "The early Americans loved George Washington for leading them through the war to become their own nation. He earned their respect and admiration after years of hard work."

"But I think we just lost our chance to ask George Washington about tips for my election," Cam said, disappointed.

"Don't worry, Cam. I'll come up with a plan B," I replied. In fact, a spark of an idea for getting one-on-one time with President Washington was already forming in my head.

Liberty made an exaggerated coughing noise and said, "Knock, knock."

I shook my head as Cam laughed. "Who's there?"

"Olive," said Liberty.

"Olive who?" asked Cam.

"Olive us should go and get some lunch—what do you say?"

I laughed and replied, "I guess it is time to go."

We found an empty alley, where I climbed up onto Liberty's saddle with Cam.

Liberty said, *"Rush, rush, rushing from history!"* and the portal opened to modern day.

This is the presidential motorcade at the inaugural parade surrounded by U.S. Secret Service. Can you see any similarities and differences from April 30, 1789?

Do you see George Washington at Federal Hall, New York, on April 30, 1789? Do you know what he is doing?

Chapter 3

We landed back in modern day at the exact same spot near the oak tree.

"I don't know about you but I am hung-ry, with a capital *H*," said Liberty.

I took another carrot out of Liberty's saddlebag and fed it to him.

"I also need a catnap. Why do they call it *catnap*, anyway? It really should be *horse nap*. I mean, horses are far more interesting than boring old cats, and we are good sleepers."

We laughed at Liberty's continual train of thought and random observations.

Cam started thinking out loud as he removed his colonial clothing from over his modern-day clothes. "When I'm President Cam, I want a big parade just like George Washington. That would be supercool."

I nodded and said, "President Washington's inauguration

was really great, wasn't it? Did you notice anything different from those days to today, other than the president's car, Air Force One, the White House, and a bunch of reporters with TV cameras? You know, those little details." I laughed, entertained by my own joke.

Cam's face showed he was in thinking mode. "I noticed there were a lot more horses cruising around the streets," he responded. "They were like taxis."

"I take offense to being called a taxi. I prefer 'equine transport extraordinaire.' Thank you very much," Liberty muttered.

"A lot of things in modern day are different due to technology, but it is amazing many of the traditions that started when President Washington was elected as the first president are still the exact same today," I said. "Maybe we could put together a field trip for our club to go to the next national presidential inauguration in January."

"That would be really fun," Cam said. "I will be president then so I will have something in common with the other president."

He seemed fairly serious.

I continued, "There are a lot of traditions started by George Washington that are still in effect today. Can you think of any?"

After a pause Cam replied, "The White House?"

"That's a good answer, but actually when George Washington was first elected Washington, D.C., was not yet the capital. So he lived in New York for a while in what was called the President's House.

"The traditions started by George Washington that are still followed by presidents today include reciting the Presidential Oath outdoors, and adding '*So help me God*' afterward. Remember that no one in history did it before George Washington, so he set the example. It is what we call a P-R-E-C-E-D-E-N-T."

"I think you mean 'president,' Revere," Liberty said, seriously.

I shook my head smiling. "The two words sound alike. I don't mean President of the United States. I mean precedent, as in something that is followed once someone does it the first time, because they respect the tradition."

Liberty nodded. "Well done, Revere. I was just testing you."

Cam looked very focused. He smiled widely and said, "Everyone was cheering for President Washington. He was the man. I mean, it was like a music concert with people screaming his name. So basically, I want to be the George Washington of Manchester Middle."

Liberty raised his eyebrows, half-listening, half-chomping.

Cam clapped his hands together. "Everyone will love me because I'll be president. And it'll be easy because everyone will love me."

I laughed. "Yes, President Washington was loved by almost everybody but not just because he was president. The people loved him for leading the Continental Army to victory and for starting our new nation independent from the King. Remember, with fame and glory comes a lot of hard work. President Washington had to make a ton of tough decisions. That is a very important part of being president."

"Oh yeah, totally," Cam agreed. "Hard work, then the Presidential Cam limo. How cool would that be? Ladies and gentlemen, President Cam has arrived." He laughed.

Even though he was saying the words, I wasn't so sure he knew how much effort and strategy would actually be involved in winning the election and then being president.

"So for you to get the title of president and win cool points, it will take some steps to get there," I said.

This is a photograph of Marine One returning to the White House with the president on board. What is the name of the president's plane?

"On it!" Cam announced as he ran toward the car pickup point.

The next afternoon, Cam practically skipped into the classroom, looking as though he had just found a twenty-dollar bill on the sidewalk. "Hello, American Adventurers," he said, smiling widely. School had just ended so we had about ten minutes until the start of the club.

Tommy glanced skeptically at his best friend and asked, "Why are you so happy?"

"I had an awesome dream last night," said Cam.

Freedom walked into the classroom, slid her backpack off her shoulder, and sat next to Cam and Tommy. She wore her hair down with a long yellow braid in front. "What are you guys talking about?" she asked.

"Cam is telling me about his awesome dream," Tommy replied.

"So I dreamt I got to see George Washington's inauguration. The whole crowd was cheering when he got up to give his Presidential Oath."

Tommy said, leaning back in his chair, "I've never had that dream. Sounds like this election thing is really stressing you out, buddy."

Freedom nodded.

Cam leaned in, spread his hands wide, and whispered, "Okay, the truth is, it wasn't a dream; that's why I'm so pumped."

Freedom and Tommy both turned to look at each other and then slowly turned to me.

"Wait a minute, you guys went without us?" Tommy asked accusingly.

Cam came to my rescue. "Sorry, man, but Mr. Revere thought maybe we could talk to George Washington about being president and get some ideas for my election. We kinda couldn't let the rest of the club know."

"Tonight, I hope you dream that you're being chased by British redcoats," teased Freedom. "Seriously though, what was it like?"

Tommy scooted his desk a little closer. "Yeah, what did you guys talk about?" he asked.

Cam shrugged his shoulders. "We didn't actually hang out like in '76 this time," Cam replied. "GW was up above us on this balcony."

"At Federal Hall," I added.

"I bet he would have worked in a *Hi Cam* if he saw me." Cam smiled.

"Maybe he didn't have enough time for shout-outs?" Tommy joked.

Cam laughed. "Yup, but it was awesome. George Washington was the man. I'm thinking I could have a big parade around school. I could give my presidential oath in front of a huge pep rally or something."

"Glad you're not getting a big head." Tommy smiled.

Cam added, "I didn't really know how all this stuff goes together. But Mr. Revere taught me that the Presidential Oath comes straight from the Constitution. Which is cool."

Tommy and Freedom nodded, looking impressed.

I was proud of Cam. It always amazed me how much the crew absorbed on these trips.

As other students entered the classroom, I interrupted and whispered, "Let's hold the time-travel discussion for later."

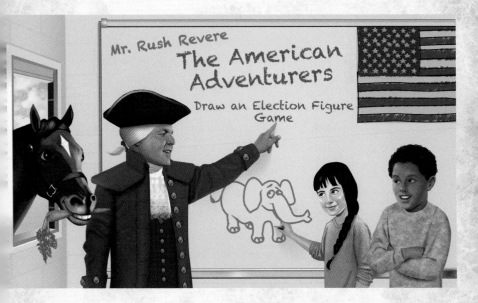

I took a deep breath and announced, "Good afternoon, everyone." The students seemed tired after the school day, but they sat up excitedly when Liberty poked his head through the open window.

"Do we have any snacks today?" a boy asked from the back of the room.

I laughed and replied, "I don't think our friend Mr. Liberty ordered any meals today. Those will just be for special occasions."

I looked over at Liberty and noticed he was trying to get my attention. He waved his head left and right, up and down, a few times in a row. He was starting to make me dizzy.

As he did, Freedom jumped up from her seat and said, "My friend and I made up a secret club handshake to go with our new name. Wanna see?"

"Absolutely!" I replied.

Freedom's friend stood up and faced her. They did a quick flutter with their hands, a few fist bumps, a wavy arch, elbow touches, a turn, and a little foot-waving dance.

"*Bravo*, very creative," I said. "Would you mind teaching everyone in the club all the moves?"

"Okay," both girls replied proudly.

Soon everyone in the club was practicing the secret handshake. Once everyone was sufficiently immersed, I took the opportunity to walk over and find out what Liberty was up to.

"What's going on?" I whispered.

Slyly, Liberty looked from side to side and muttered softly, "The eagle has landed."

"What?" I said, glancing over my shoulder, hoping our conversation was going unnoticed.

"The sparrow has laid an egg," Liberty said.

"What are you talking about?" I asked, confused.

Liberty rolled his eyes. "Your package has been delivered."

"Oh, you mean the thing I rented for today's lesson?" I said, catching on.

Liberty exhaled strongly. "Yes, sheesh, you would have made a terrible spy."

I ignored his comment and said, "I need you to pull it over onto the grass behind the school. Can you do that? I told the delivery company to just leave it in the most convenient place this afternoon and we would take care of the rest."

"No problemo, Capitán!" said Liberty, attempting a salute.

"Just signal when everything is set up," I said. "And make sure it has water. And yes, I know this will cost me extra bagels."

"Oh, you know it will," said Liberty, trotting away.

I quickly made my way back to the front of the class and said, "All right, Tommy and Freedom, let's see the new secret handshake for our club."

"Okay, we'll show you in slow motion so it's easy to see," said Tommy. "Then, real fast."

I nodded sincerely.

After the handshake demonstration, Tommy announced, "And that's the American Adventurers secret club handshake."

The other club members applauded with me, except for Cam. He was feverishly writing in his playbook and didn't seem to be paying too much attention to what was going on around him.

"Let's have everyone stand up here at the front of the room and practice together," I said. "Then you can split into groups of two. On the count of three let's do one full class secret hand-shake. You too, Cam."

Cam heard his name and looked up from his paper. "Secret Service?" he asked.

"Secret handshake," I clarified, raising my eyebrows.

"Oh yeah. No problem. Absolutely, I'm in."

Freedom motioned for Cam to join her. "Cam, I'll practice with you."

"Okay, cool. Thanks, Freedom." Cam left his notebook on his desk and joined her.

I observed the club from the front corner of the room. They were all counting down at different times as they slapped, bumped, and clapped the secret handshake. I was just close enough to eavesdrop on Cam and Freedom's conversation.

"Thanks for helping me, Freedom," Cam said. "I was busy taking notes about George Washington's inauguration and my party plans for when I win. I'm thinking of grilling hot dogs and hamburgers."

"*When* you win?" Freedom teased. "Don't you mean *if* you win?"

"No, *when* I win," Cam asserted. "I've totally got this. All I have to do is get some people to vote for me and I'll be the most popular guy in school, just like Washington. If he could do it, I can. No problem."

Freedom raised one eyebrow and then rolled her eyes.

"Okay, American Adventurers," I said, "time is up. I'm eager to see all the handshakes on the count of three. . . ."

Liberty poked his head through the window again and gave me a wink and a nod. I assumed this meant things were ready outside for our history game.

Turning back to the room, I continued, "Okay, here we go. On the count of three. One, two, three . . . go!"

Hands flew everywhere in unison.

"Awesome job!" I cheered.

There were smiles and high-fives all around as the students sat back down at their desks.

Out of nowhere, Cam sprang to his feet and exclaimed, "Ladies and gentlemen, may I have your attention, please?"

The club all turned to him.

Cam cleared his throat and read from a sheet of paper. "I am announcing my candidacy for student body president. Everyone will love me, just like George Washington." He paused to look around the room, smiling widely.

The rest of the club looked at him, confused.

Cam continued reading: "I ask for your vote. I will be the best president around. Here's to me, President Cam of Manchester Middle School. Make sure you get to know me now, because when I'm president I'll be busy with more important things, so I won't have time."

There was silence in the room for mere seconds, but it felt much longer.

After getting over Cam's unexpected announcement, I said, "Let's give a round of applause to the new Manchester Middle School presidential candidate—Cam."

Tommy clapped loudly, and the other students eventually followed.

Freedom half-smiled and said uneasily, "That's great Cam, congratulations."

Cam raced up to me at the teacher's desk and asked, "How did I do? I feel more popular already!"

"You surprised me with your impromptu speech but good job being courageous. Let's talk a little more after this club meeting about your campaign strategy. I think we should talk about the next steps and your goals for the school as student body president."

"Okay, that sounds easy enough," Cam replied eagerly, and headed back to his seat. He was so sure he was going to win easily, I was getting nervous for him. He seemed a little ahead of himself.

Tommy looked on intently and raised his hand. "Mr. Revere, now that we have our club name and our handshake, what are we going to do next?"

"Great question, thank you, Tommy," I replied. "So, you all know there is a national presidential election happening, as well as a Manchester Middle School election as Cam just confirmed. In honor of both elections, and the future presidents, I think we should play a game I call *Presidential Election Splashdown*." It was the first name that came to me.

"*Presidential Splashdown?*" said the brown-haired girl near Freedom.

"Is that like presidents in the ocean?" Tommy joked.

I laughed. "To start, I'll need a volunteer. Someone who is brave and daring, like a good leader."

Cam quickly raised his hand. "I'll do it. I mean, if President George Washington were here I'd bet he'd do it. But since he isn't, I'm happy to step into his presidential shoes."

"Thank you, Cam," I said, grinning. "Now, let's all go outside to the grassy field behind the school where Liberty is waiting."

All the club members looked intrigued and excited as they filed out of the room.

When we met up with Liberty, the curiosity meter was at ultrahigh. Liberty was standing next to a dunk tank—a giant blue bucket with a large plastic window on the side of it. It was easy to see that the dunk tank was filled with water. The tank was taller than Tommy and wide enough to fit half our club members inside. A soft, plastic seat hovered about a foot and a half above the water and was connected to a lever that was attached to a metal arm that extended out from the back of the tank to about two feet to the right of the bucket. A target with a painted bull's-eye the size of a small dinner plate was attached to the other end of the metal arm. Finally, a wire cage surrounded the front side, obviously meant to protect whoever would be sitting on the collapsing chair.

"Before I answer your questions, let me explain how this game will work," I said. "I will ask you a question about United States presidents or the election process. The first student to raise his or her hand with the correct answer will receive a ball and a chance to throw it at the bull's-eye. I think you all know what happens when you hit the bull's-eye."

Cam's arm shot up. "Mr. Revere, I volunteered to throw the ball, right?"

I gave him my most sympathetic face and replied, "Oh, no, Cam. You volunteered to be confident and brave just like George Washington. You'll have an opportunity to show your fellow students and future voters what it means to be a true leader."

"That's what I was afraid of," Cam said, gulping.

"Go get 'em, Cam," said Tommy, enthusiastically. "You did say you wanted to be just like George WASH-ington." He slapped Cam on the back and busted up, laughing.

"Whatever," Cam said. Like a good sport, he walked around

the back of the dunk tank, climbed up, and carefully sat on the small plastic seat. "I wish I had my bathing suit."

Liberty whinnied with delight.

"Please give me the first ball—*please*," Tommy begged. "I've been practicing my spiral!"

"All right, listen carefully for your chance to win a ball," I said. "Here we go. I'll start out with an easy one. In what month does the presidential election occur in the United States?"

Tommy shouted, "Hey, Cam, throw me your shoes and socks so at least they don't get wet!" He started laughing before he even finished his sentence.

"Actually, that's a good idea," Cam said, and he carefully took off his shoes and socks and threw them to the side.

"This is an easy one, Mr. Revere," Tommy answered. "November."

"Oh, that is the correct answer, November, but you did not raise your hand," I said, half chuckling.

Tommy snapped his fingers, laughing. "Aw, c'mon, Mr. Revere."

"Okay, here we go, question number two. It's a little harder than the first: In the United States who votes for the president and what gives them the ability to vote?" I looked out at a sea of wide-eyed students.

A young brunette with her hair in a ponytail and a bright green T-shirt raised her hand and said, "I know!"

"Go ahead, the floor is yours," I said.

The young girl replied confidently, "The people of the United States have the right to vote. It is from the Constitution."

I clapped. "Absolutely correct, extremely well done. Americans have the freedom to vote for the president of their choice. The Founding Fathers wanted to ensure the presidency would be by the people and for the people, not the rule of a king." I passed the girl with the correct answer a ball and said, "Here you go. You get the first throw."

Cam shouted, "I'm confident you aren't going to hit the bull's-eye 'cause I'm not feeling like a bath right now!"

Everyone laughed. The girl wound up as if she were about to throw a fastball pitch. The ball brushed the side of the target just enough to rattle Cam's chair but not drop him into the tank.

"Oh, you got lucky, Cam!" Freedom shouted, smiling.

Cam yelled, "It's not luck, Freedom. Leaders like me use skill!"

Freedom replied, "I hope one of your skills is swimming because you're going to need it."

"Oh, ladies and gentlemen, Freedom is in the house," said Tommy.

Freedom started laughing.

Liberty was off to the side, munching on a carrot stick as if he were eating popcorn and watching a great movie.

"Okay, are you ready?" I asked. "Next question: When two candidates go on TV and talk about their ideas or answer questions from the moderator, what is it called?"

Freedom's hand shot up quickly. When I called on her, she paused for a second. I could tell the answer was on the tip of her tongue.

"Any day now," Tommy joked.

"Sorry, sorry, I know it: a *debate*," she replied.

"Absolutely correct. Throughout the election season there are many presidential debates on TV. This is when the candidates tell the voters what their ideas are or answer questions about themselves so that the voters get to know them better.

Sometimes the candidates argue with each other," I said, passing the ball to Freedom.

She wound up and threw the ball as fast as she could. It glided through the air, barely missing Cam's head.

"Hey, hey, I thought we were friends. You almost took me out!" Cam joked, while shaking a fist at Freedom.

"All right, let me change my line of questioning a little. Who can tell us the names of the first three presidents of the United States?" I asked.

Cam blurted out from his perch above the water, "George Washington became first president of the United States to be the man. The coolest guy in the land."

"What happened to raising your hand and being called on to answer?" I said. "Since Cam partially answered that one, the first three presidents of the United States were George Washington, John Adams, and Thomas Jefferson. Moving on to the next question . . ."

We were just getting warmed up, when I heard the sound of a familiar voice.

"Mr. Revere, what exactly are you doing?" Principal Sherman stood with both hands on his hips. He looked at me with focused eyes, clearly not impressed with the dunk tank.

"Oh, hello, Principal Sherman. We are playing a game about our presidential election process and talking about great presidents from history."

I looked around and couldn't see Liberty anywhere. I was relieved and hoped that Principal Sherman hadn't seen him. I had enough explaining to do with the dunk tank.

"Mr. Revere, we cannot have large tanks of water on school

grounds," Principal Sherman said, shutting down our Presidential Splashdown afternoon.

He turned on his heel and walked off. "Mr. Revere, meet me inside."

When Principal Sherman had reentered the school, Cam raised both hands over his head and yelled, "Victory! Oh, yeah, I'm invincible just like George Wash—"

Before he could finish his sentence, something *invisible* hit the bull's-eye and Cam dropped like an anchor into the tank.

"Presidential Splashdown!" Tommy yelled, laughing.

The rest of the club cheered.

Cam's head popped up out of the water. Thankfully, he was smiling as he yelled, "Liberty!"

As the rest of the club ran to the tank to help Cam, Liberty reappeared at my side and said, "So, ummm, maybe you shoulda asked Principal Sherman before. Get clearance, yunno?"

"You had to hit the bull's-eye?" I asked.

"Yep, I had to," Liberty said. "Those kids were so disappointed when Principal Sherman shut you down. Plus, Cam needed to know that he is not invincible."

Liberty did have a point. And seeing Cam laughing with the other club members was definitely a bonding moment. Maybe this was turning out to be a good thing. Well, except for my upcoming visit to the principal's office.

"Okay, everyone, it looks like our club meeting is over for today. We will continue the fun tomorrow." We headed back to the classroom to gather our belongings.

Cam came running up behind me, dripping wet. He said, "Hey, Mr. Revere, when should I make my announcement to the school? I think I totally know what to do. Totally got it."

Cam actually seemed reenergized by the splashdown. I continued walking and said, "I really think we need to talk some more about your plan. I have to go inside to talk to Principal Sherman. Why don't you wait here with Liberty and I'll catch up with you as soon as I can? And Liberty has your colonial clothing if you want to dry off."

"No worries," said Cam. "I have some extra sweats and stuff in my locker."

"Oh, good. Well, I'll see you shortly, I hope." I turned to enter the school.

Gratefully, my visit with Principal Sherman was short. After promising not to have any more dunk tanks on school grounds, I walked back outside to find Cam, Tommy, and Freedom all gathered under the large oak tree, with Liberty hovering over their shoulders.

I overheard Cam say, "Everyone should vote for me. I think that splashdown proved I'm a born leader. I'm totally funny, pretty good-looking, have a nice smile, and I'm an all-around good guy."

I looked at him with my eyebrows raised.

Cam said, "Seriously, how hard can it be to win?"

"Cam, your run for president just got a lot harder," Freedom said, looking nervous.

Liberty nodded. "Don't look now. Yes, do look. No, don't look, yes, do look."

"Look at what?" I asked. I followed Liberty's wide-eyed stare and looked behind me.

"Oh no," I said.

"What?" Cam said, turning around. "Ugh, you have got to be kidding me." His confident smile suddenly faded.

Straight across the grass courtyard in plain view, a half circle of girls were gathering together like at a mini Taylor Swift concert.

"No way," Cam said. "I cannot believe this."

"What is it, Cam? All I see is a bunch of girls in the courtyard. What's wrong?" I asked.

Someone was in the center of the group, and they were all jumping up and down around her. At first I could not make out who it was. Then I saw her long blond hair.

Standing higher than all of the other girls was Elizabeth. She was holding a large paper sign that read ELIZABETH FOR PRESIDENT.

Chapter 9

Cam put his hands on his head and paced back and forth. "This is a disaster," he said. "Elizabeth cannot be running for president. She is so irritating and doesn't even want it. I know she's just doing it to annoy me. Remember that day in the hallway when she told me it was totally dumb?"

Freedom stood silently, looking concerned.

Cam appeared more frustrated by the second. He was clearly not taking the news of Elizabeth running against him well.

All of a sudden an idea popped into my head. We had a secret agent right next to us who could find out all of the intel. I looked Liberty in the eye so he would focus. "Liberty, it's time for you to go into stealth mode," I said. "Your mission is to visit Elizabeth's gathering and discover as much as you can about what she is planning."

"Roger that, Captain," said Liberty. "On the case. Consider it done. Stealth mode activated." Liberty inhaled deeply, held his breath, and vanished from our eyes.

Cam groaned. "If she becomes president she'll act like the Queen of Manchester Middle. I mean, she'll probably change our cool lion mascot into a pink kitten or something stupid."

"There's no way she's going to win, Cam," said Freedom. "Elizabeth cuts everyone down and makes them feel badly about themselves. Nobody wants to vote for a mean president."

I was at a loss. I didn't want to be negative, but I was concerned about Elizabeth's motives. It's possible she wanted to run for president for the right reasons, but I doubted it.

Freedom said, "Liberty is coming back from his mission. I can feel him getting closer."

Seconds later, Liberty reappeared in front of us. He was panting like he had just run a marathon, but it was likely for dramatic effect.

"So, what did you find out?" I asked.

Cam and Freedom walked closer. "Yeah, what is Eliza-brat doing now?" Cam asked.

"Okay, okay, here's the skinny, the 411, the up-to-the-minute breaking news information," Liberty said. I looked at him seriously, hoping to hurry his thoughts along.

"Elizabeth is definitely running for president, no doubt," he said, taking a deep breath. "The rest of her sign says 'Vote for Me, I'm the Best—You'll See!'"

"Ugh, totally unfair," said Cam, shaking his head. "She's going to ruin the school. She'll probably let all the cheerleaders have hall passes and make us drink kale smoothies."

George Washington as Commander of the Continental Army, greeted by happy crowds as he entered New York City in 1783.

"Oh, I like kale," said Liberty. "It is very good for you. It is the best vitamin-packed wonder food of all time. Makes my mouth water just thinking about it."

Freedom nudged Liberty and whispered, "You're not helping."

"Oops, sorry," he said. "My bad. But kale really is yummy."

Cam's face was red and serious. "I'm just so mad."

Liberty and I arrived outside Boston Bagels early in the morning. I suggested to Cam that we meet there before school to think about his election strategy. The shop was buzzing with patrons enjoying their coffee and bagels. The front tables were packed, and a line formed to the counter. A tall woman sidestepped past me, talking on her cell phone, carrying a large cup of coffee. There was movement everywhere.

Just as I was about to peek inside I heard someone call my name. "Mr. Revere!" Cam shouted. I turned to see him getting out of his mother's car. As I waved, she told him to be careful crossing the parking lot. I had told her earlier by phone that I would make sure he was at school on time.

A couple got up from a table around the corner from the main entrance and we grabbed it.

I whispered into Liberty's ear, "We'll come back out after we order so we can all sit together. If anyone asks, I'll say you're a police horse or a circus pony. I'm still deciding which."

"Very funny, Revere, very funny," Liberty said, looking unimpressed. "Don't forget I'm a growing horse. I need at least two bagels to get the motor running."

I smiled as I followed Cam into the bagel shop. "Have you been here before?" I asked.

"Yeah, before my dad left this time, he took me here before school." He shrugged his shoulders.

"That's great," I replied, hoping we hadn't made a bad decision picking this spot for our morning brainstorming session. I didn't want to make Cam feel any worse that his father was away.

I was relieved when Cam happily said, "The cheese bagel sandwich is really good. And the hot chocolate with extra marshmallows is awesome."

"I'm glad you guys decided to meet up before class. I think it will really help your campaign. Your big speech and the vote are about three weeks away now, right?" I asked.

Cam nodded contentedly.

As we stood in line waiting to place our order, I glanced out the large glass window at the front of the shop. A flash of brown caught my eye. It was Liberty, hopping from one hoof to the next, as if he were dancing. I thought he was either guarding the table, shooing away stray birds, or practicing for a TV dancing show.

"What is Liberty doing?" Cam asked, smirking. He started to hop on one foot and the other, copying Liberty.

I laughed and replied, "That is the million-dollar question, isn't it?"

We picked up our warm bagels and walked outside. On the way, a distinguished, gray-haired gentleman wearing a perfectly ironed blue polo, khaki pants, and brown loafers said, "Good morning, young man. Great to see you again. How's your pop?"

Cam half-smiled and mumbled, "He's good," but kept walking toward the door.

I paused and said, "Good morning," to the man, trying not to be rude. He surprisingly didn't look at all fazed by my colonial outfit.

"I notice you have your horse with you. He is a good-looking one," the man said. "Must be a show horse if he can stand at a bagel shop like this."

"Thank you, he is a character, that's for sure. My name is Rush Revere," I said, holding out my hand.

The man shook my hand firmly and said, "My name is Joseph. It is a pleasure to meet you."

"I'm Cam's history teacher. I'm helping him with his election campaign. You could say this is our campaign headquarters."

"Is he running for president of the United States? Don't you still have to be thirty-five years old? Cam looks great for his age," Joseph joked.

I laughed. "Actually, he is running for student body president of Manchester Middle School, down the road there." I looked at Cam, who was outside at our table, happily drinking his hot chocolate and playing with his phone. I added, "Not quite the national presidential election, I suppose, but there are certain similarities."

Joseph smiled. "I know a bit about elections myself. I used to be a U.S. congressman. But that was a few years ago and a lot has changed."

"That is incredible," I said. "It is a real honor to meet you. I am particularly fascinated by the history of Congress and the United States government."

I looked out the window again and saw Cam eagerly waving me over.

"Pardon me, Congressman, but we have to get back to Cam's election strategy before school starts."

"Sounds good. Let me know if Cam ever needs any campaign advice." He smiled and turned to get in line.

When I reached the table, Cam had already unwrapped his breakfast bagel and was halfway done. "I still can't believe Elizabeth is running for president," Cam said.

Purposely changing the subject, I asked, "Do you know that nice man inside?"

"Not really. I used to see him whenever my dad and I came here," Cam replied. "He and my dad used to talk a lot. Seriously, though, what's up with Elizabeth? Totally unfair!"

Liberty stopped chomping on his spinach bagel to add, "Well, life is not fair, my friend, trust me. If it were I could fly first class instead of coach."

"You can't fly coach, either. You're a horse. You *pull* coaches," I joked.

"See what I mean?" Liberty snorted. "Totally unfair." He pretended to cry, melodramatic as usual.

Ignoring Liberty, I took a sip of coffee and pulled out a list of notes, including Cam's email about why he wants to be president.

"So, Cam, you said you want to be class president to be popular, to be called *President Cam*, make up new school rules, and tell Elizabeth what to do. Right?" I said, reading down the list.

Cam nodded, smiling. "Yep, that's pretty much it—sounds good."

I smiled. "Okay, so that's a start. But there are a few things you are missing. To get votes, you need to think about what specific things you would do for the students if you became student body president. How are your ideas different and better than Elizabeth's or the other candidates'?" I paused to think of a good example. "So you know in the current national presidential election, each candidate has a position on a particular subject? In the TV commercials or debates, one of the candidates focuses on education, for example, while the other is focused on lowering taxes?"

Cam nodded, "I think so."

"So you already know you want to be cool like George Washington. Now you need to decide what you want to achieve as president. In other words, how do you plan to improve Manchester Middle School?"

Cam shrugged.

I pointed at Cam's notebook on the table. "Start by writing this down in your playbook. You already completed what we can call plays one and two. Play one was to *find out the rules and criteria for running for student body president*. Play two was to *decide you are running, sign up, and determine what you would do as president*."

"Got it, Mr. Revere. I like having plays to plan out." He wrote the plays in his notebook and marked each as *completed*.

"I will think of some more as we go along," I said.

Liberty tapped his hoof on the floor and shimmied like he was trying to shake off fleas. "Wait, wait, I have another superduper idea. Why don't you make me your campaign advisor? I already picked this bagel-heaven campaign headquarters, making me the most qualified applicant."

Cam laughed and said, "Um, okay, Liberty."

"Hey, hey, I'm serious here. I've been thinking about this for a while and I have a lot of stored-up genius. I'm basically bursting with winning ideas."

I smiled and looked at Cam's list. "So, in addition to coolness, what will you do as president to help your fellow students?"

Cam put his right hand under his chin. "I'm not sure. Maybe we could have half-day Fridays."

Right then, Liberty jumped in. "I've got it. Thank you very much. I'm probably not getting paid my due as campaign advisor because this is *brilliant* to the horse degree."

"Okay, Liberty. Please, tell us your brilliant idea," I said skeptically.

Liberty explained: "We all know Washington was cool, and Cam wants to be cool like him. But call me crazy—what if it takes more than being cool to become president? What if it takes a lot of work to get there, like taking knots out of my mane? I bet if we go and visit GW again, he could tell us what he did to become president."

He paused and looked around, expectantly.

"Liberty, that *is* brilliant," I said, clapping my hands. "Going back in time again to speak with George Washington about being president is exactly what we should do. Following Cam's playbook we can ask him how he decided to become president, and what were his plans for the country. Perfect for election strategy and leadership if Cam wins."

Cam agreed. "Oh, I'm going to win, Mr. Revere, no doubt."

We made plans to time-travel, right after the American Adventurers club meeting.

Cam, Liberty, and I met at the tree after the club meeting.

"Unfortunately, Freedom and Tommy will not be able to join us," I said. "Tommy has to leave early for team pictures and Freedom was going to be picked up early for a hair trim."

Cam looked excited and said, "I thought of a bunch of questions for George Washington and have them right here in my playbook."

"Way to go, Cam," I said enthusiastically. "Don't forget to put it in Liberty's saddlebag."

"Speaking of go, let's get going!" Liberty yelled, bouncing on his hooves.

I shook my head, smiled, and said, "May 27, 1790, Cherry Street Mansion, New York City."

Liberty opened the yellow and purple time portal and we *rush, rush, rushed to history.*

After jumping through the portal, we were only minutes from arriving in front of a beautiful three-story square building. A horse-drawn carriage passed carrying a man in a formal jacket. It was a warm, sunny day. Tall, thin trees shaded parts of the old road in front of the house.

"I thought we were going to Washington, D.C. How are we supposed to get election tips if we don't go to the White House?" Cam said with a sour look.

"The building in front of us is called the Cherry Street Mansion. It is where President Washington lived after his inauguration. It may not be the White House, but it is where the president lived in 1790," I replied.

Large windows framed the front door of the mansion, and there were two floors with five sets of windows each. On either side were similar-sized houses.

"Cool," Cam replied.

People entered the house, carrying plates and silverware.

"You don't just walk into the President's House," I warned. "Just like in modern day, you need to make an appointment."

"Makes sense," Cam replied. "They look like they are having a party or something."

"And everybody knows a party means food!" Liberty yelled, causing a passing woman in a velvet dress to drop her fan to the ground.

As we neared the front door I began to say, "Now, let me think about how to get inside . . ." when a grandmotherly woman with white hair, in a gold dress and lace cap, came out the front door. She was directing traffic and moving people this way and that.

"Don't just stand there," she said, with a bright smile. She was small in stature, but forceful in her movements. She looked directly at me. "Sir, take your horse around to the side and help me bring in the apples and the wine for tonight."

"Yes, ma'am," I said.

Cam looked at me with a cautious glance and mouthed, "What are we doing?"

"We're in luck," I said. "We just met the *First Lady*, Mrs. Martha Washington. This is our chance to get inside the mansion," I said.

We walked around to the side of the house near a large swinging door. Liberty followed closely behind. I spotted the apple crates and took off my coat. "Cam, if I carry the apples, can you grab the wine?"

"Sure, no problem," replied Cam.

The apples were heavier than they looked.

Liberty managed to avoid any kind of manual labor and pounced on a loose apple, swallowing it whole.

"Okay, follow me, Cam, we are in." We carried our boxes into the large house. The furniture inside was neatly arranged. Mrs. Washington stood in the center of a large room, supervising workers as they moved furniture.

She shook her head and said, "There is simply not enough time to host a formal dinner for the president of the United States. Everyone is so fashionable here in New York, it's impossible. At home at Mount Vernon I would be able to organize this dinner in half the time. Here the traditions are different and it takes time to figure out all the local customs. Sometimes I wish we were back home where I was comfortable."

As Mrs. Washington spoke, a tall African-American man entered the room. He had long limbs and strong arms. He looked at Cam suspiciously and said, "Where are you taking that wine, young man?" He wore a serious expression.

"Uh, I was just going to put it over there by the wall," Cam replied, nervously.

The man barked, "You need to take the wine into the wine cellar. Those who serve it will take it into the main dining room. The party is starting in a few minutes."

"Sorry, I don't really know anything about wine. I'm not old enough," Cam said.

"Don't know about wine?" the man shouted. He wore a dark brown coat, neatly tailored, and his hair long. His face looked tired and wrinkled. As he walked I noticed a stoop in his shoulders and his knees wobbled. He grabbed the box from Cam and gave it to another man to take to the wine cellar.

Cam froze. Just then the man laughed loudly. He grabbed his stomach and his voice bounced off the ivory walls. "You may not know about wine, but you better know about work, so say 'yes, sir' and do what you are told."

He began laughing again, patted Cam on the shoulder, pointed to another box, and said, "Take that box there and get your clothes on for tonight. We need someone to tie up the horses when the guests come." Cam nodded gravely.

The man ushered us into the kitchen and gave Cam a dress coat. "Guests are arriving. Head out front and handle the horses, young man," he said, then turned and left.

Just then, two children, a boy and a girl, came bounding into the kitchen. "Are you helping with the horses?" the young boy asked.

"Oh hey, sure," Cam replied.

"I'm Wash and this is my sister, Nelly. What's your name?"

Cam looked back at me with his eyebrows raised. "I'm Cam. I like your house. It's kinda huge."

"It's our grandparents' house," the older girl named Nelly said. "It's fun to run around, but there's always a lot of adults."

"That sounds cool," Cam replied. He was tugging on his old-fashioned collar.

"It's kind of warm actually, not really cool at all," the boy named Wash said. His reddish hair was messy and flowing, and he wore a high-collared shirt.

"Ignore him, it's just fine in here, nice and cool, yes." Nelly shook her head.

Cam smiled and said, "What's it like having your grandparents as the President and Mrs. President?"

Formally, Nelly replied, "I think it is quite wonderful, actually. There are lots of levees, or parties, to attend with my grandparents, and I am able to wear lovely clothes. Usually, we leave early, but it is still quite enjoyable." Nelly was wearing a flowing white dress that appeared to be made completely of lace. Her reddish hair was styled up in the front and then flowing down her shoulders. As she spoke, her dainty fingers turned up like a gymnast's.

Cam's cheeks turned red as she spoke and he looked at her with a warm expression.

"Is it great to have George Washington as your grandpa? Everyone loves him and stuff." He fidgeted in his jacket.

Nelly, standing up straight, with one leg pointing forward gracefully, replied, "Oh, he is the best grandfather in the world. We do not see him very often because he is always working, but when we do he is really kind and plays with us. He makes up these games where we go to the woods and explore. He takes out the map and we have to find exactly where we are."

Wash blabbered, "Oh, yeah, that's so fun, we get muddy and wet in the rain, and then we get lost, and Grandpa finds us and helps us and the horses come and we run around."

"Our grandfather spent years mapping out the countryside, and it helped him during the Revolutionary War," Nelly said, intelligently. "Sometimes Grandpa gets frustrated as president but he always calms down when Grandma touches his arm. Then he smiles at us. It's nice to be here."

Wash grabbed Cam's arm and said, "Let's go help with the horses so we can play after."

"Um, okay," Cam said.

I whispered to Cam, "Please be sure to stick to Nelly and Wash like glue and don't leave the mansion grounds." I was nervous to let Cam out of my sight for long, but he nodded reassuringly and the three walked out through the kitchen door together toward the stables.

I finished helping with the boxes and put my blue coat back on. Unsure where to go next, I returned to the large room and looked around. I wondered where Liberty was and hoped he wasn't getting into trouble.

Martha Washington was the first first lady of the United States.
She cared for the troops at Valley Forge.

George Washington was the first president of the United States. He led the
American forces against the mighty British superpower.

Just then, President Washington entered the room. He was wearing dark boots, stockings, and a black velvet suit. It was like seeing the main star in a movie for the first scene. My heart raced. Did I make a mistake letting Cam run off with Nelly and Wash? Would he miss the moment to speak with President Washington about his election? I took a deep breath and composed myself. *Act cool, Revere*, I thought.

"What is all this blasted noise? What is going on in here?" President Washington growled. He seemed annoyed, unlike when we previously met each other, in 1776. Washington scanned the room quickly, like a military officer looking over his troops. All of a sudden, he paused and looked intensely at me. I panicked, realizing I had no idea what to say.

He raised his hand and firmly said, "I demand to know what is happening here. Who is in charge?"

Mrs. Washington appeared out of a side room and announced, "We are preparing for tonight's levee, dear. There isn't much time before the guests arrive, and we must finish the final touches." She turned away from her husband, and instructed several men on remaining chores.

President Washington's face warmed. "Very well," he sighed, and turned to walk out of the room.

I followed behind.

"Excuse me, Mr. President," I called out. He paused and turned around.

"I apologize for bothering you, sir, I know you are busy."

President Washington stopped. His presence was larger than life. He looked at me without blinking.

"I am Rush Revere," I said, trying my best to remain composed. "We met during the war, in 1776."

His face lit up in recognition. "Mr. Revere? Why of course. It has been quite some time."

"Thank you, Mr. President, it has indeed." I bowed deeply. It was customary to bow rather than shake hands at the time.

How am I going to find an excuse for always being in the right place at the right time? I thought. Telling President Washington a long-winded tale about time travel was certainly not an option.

"Where have you been all these years?" President Washington asked, looking skeptically at me.

"It is quite a long story, I am afraid; too long to waste your precious time."

"Thank you for that," the President replied.

I knew he was extraordinarily busy, with great demands on his time. I wondered how many people bugged him every day.

He relaxed his shoulders slightly and said, "I don't mean to be rude, but I must get some air. I do not much enjoy the commotion in the house. Would you care to join me?"

For a moment, I was frozen in shock that the president of the United States had invited me to talk further. I knew that's why we were there, but it was still thrilling.

"Why certainly, sir, I would be honored," I replied.

We walked through the house and toward the courtyard. President Washington continued to observe the hubbub surrounding him. His commanding presence could be felt in every step.

Soon after we reached the courtyard, Nelly, Wash, and Cam raced by at top speed. They didn't look like they were helping with the horses.

"I believe they have two speeds: fast and faster," President Washington said, smiling.

Nelly, Wash, and Cam in front of the Cherry Street Mansion.

I nodded, silently observing the scene. The courtyard was peaceful and surrounded by neatly cut trees and bushes. Flowers in pots contrasted with the bright white walls of the house. A light breeze swept over us as we stood in the shade of a tree, watching the three run back and forth over the tiled ground.

President Washington smiled and said, "I do not have children of my own by birth. Nelly and Wash are my adopted grandchildren, and they bring me great joy. One of my favorite things in this life is to hear their observations of the world."

"That is so very true," I said. "My students challenge me to see the world in a new way."

"Are you still a teacher? Please refresh my memory. Did I meet some of your students years ago?" President Washington asked. I was amazed he could recall this fact after so many years.

"Yes, sir, I am, and I have a group of students who are learning about American government."

President Washington said, "Young people must be educated in the science of government. They will guard liberty in the future and there is nothing more important than that."

Cam ran over to me and said energetically, "Hey, Mr. Revere, Nelly and Wash had to go inside and get cleaned up." He casually turned to see who I was speaking with and said, "Whoa, it's you." His jaw dropped open in recognition of President Washington.

"You look very familiar, young man. Have we met?" President Washington asked. He stared at Cam with a serious expression.

"Um, hello, Mr. President," he said, shyly. His eyes darted between the President and me.

I didn't know how to explain the fact that Cam was the same boy he met more than fourteen years before. I decided best not to go into detail. I pulled Cam toward me and put my hand on his shoulder so we were both facing the President.

"Cam is my student, and he often travels with me," I said.

"Thank you for helping to entertain my grandchildren, Cam," said the President.

"Uh, yeah, sure," said Cam.

"Cam is a big admirer of yours, sir. He is running for president at his school," I said. Cam looked at me with his eyebrows raised.

"Well done, young man. Being president is certainly not easy but it is an honor that the people have chosen you as their leader," President Washington said, nodding at Cam.

Cam's eyes were wide. "Sir, why did you want to be president?"

He paused, looking directly at Cam with his blue-gray eyes, and replied, "Well, I suppose the obvious answer would be for the prestige. Am I correct in saying so? For the fame and glory?"

I remained quiet.

"It is a long story, but I will answer as briefly as I know how. I lost my father when I was young. Unlike many who accuse me of wanting to become a king, I know real hardship. Nothing was handed to me. My mother did not have the means so I was unable to receive a gentleman's education, to attend college," he said.

I stayed perfectly still, listening. Cam stood beside me.

"I suppose at first I did wish for glory. I served in the French and Indian War. My horses were shot from under me and it was a vicious battle."

The early evening air was crisp as President Washington spoke. "But as the years went on, the glory became less and less important to me. I realized that my duty to my troops and later to my country and our people was far more valuable than any personal gain I had earlier hoped to achieve."

Cam turned to look up at me and then to the President.

"Mr. President, do you like being president?" Cam asked, innocently.

He paused a moment. "I cannot say that I do, in truth. It is my great and sole desire to live in peace in retirement on my farm, Mount Vernon. There I would care for my business, my family, and my household. I wish to pass an unclouded evening after the stormy day of life in the bosom of domestic tranquility. But the duty to my country bids me to serve, and I must defer to that duty. Integrity and firmness is all that I can promise."

I was speechless.

"Thank you so much for being our first president. You are my hero," Cam finally said.

"And you are a fine young man."

Just then, a female voice called out from the house. "George, please come inside, the guests are arriving. There is lemonade inside for the children."

"I'd love some lemonade, I'm thirsty," said Cam.

We walked toward the house.

"My wife is able to do so much at once," President Washington said. "No matter what the duties of the household or presidency, she always makes time for these children. She was not thrilled perhaps to move from our home at Mount Vernon, but she has been at my side throughout my life and career. During the Revolutionary War, she comforted me greatly in the darkest moments. She is a true friend, and I count on her absolutely."

At the door, the President turned to me and bowed with great dignity. "Mr. Revere, you are a man of good quality and it has been a pleasure to speak with you again. I tell the children, they must always associate themselves with people of good quality, as it is better to be alone than in bad company." President Washington turned and entered the house. I knew it would be best for me to hang back and give him some time alone.

"Cam," I said, "can you believe what we just experienced?"

"Yeah, that was awesome. Totally cool," Cam said, excitedly.

"It really was, wasn't it? I feel like I need to pinch myself to make sure it was real."

"It was definitely real, and Nelly and Wash are really fun."

"Remember to write down all of what you experienced in your playbook when we meet up with Liberty. By the way, have you seen Liberty?" I asked.

Cam shook his head.

I hoped Liberty was behaving himself.

I followed Cam as he hurried into the house to join Nelly and Wash, who were sipping lemonade at a small table. The room had filled with party guests. Everyone was dressed in fine attire. Women waved fabric fans that matched their dresses and spoke with one another. Well-dressed men stood in circles drinking from small glasses.

At first, I didn't recognize anyone and wondered what I would say if anyone asked who we were. I stayed off to the side to keep an eye on Cam and work on an excuse.

I soon noticed Mrs. Washington sitting on a fancy sofa not far from me. She sat up straight and spoke with each person as they entered. She smiled broadly. Directly next to her was another woman with dark brown hair. I concentrated on her face and soon realized it was Mrs. Abigail Adams, the wife of the Vice President.

Even though I had time-traveled many times before and met famous people, I still churned with excitement. From all I had read, Abigail Adams was a dominant force in her own right. Her husband was John Adams, and he was soon to become the second president of the United States!

I was stuck in a trance when Cam tugged on my coat and said, "Mr. Revere, I think we'd better check on Liberty."

"Okay, lead the way."

Cam started off toward the door and I followed. We passed right by the sofa where Mrs. Washington and Mrs. Adams were sitting.

"Mr. Revere," said a familiar voice.

I turned to see Mrs. Washington smiling in my direction. I paused.

"Mrs. Washington, it is a pleasure." I bowed.

"Mr. Revere, my husband tells me you engaged in a lovely conversation outside."

"Yes, we did. It was a true honor for me and my student," I replied.

"Please, let me introduce you to our guests," Mrs. Washington said, listing the names. Each person nodded. ". . . and this is Mrs. Adams."

Abigail Adams looked at me with piercing, intelligent brown eyes. She wore a thoughtful smile. Her face was bright and pale, and her dark hair was partly covered with a stylish bonnet. The arms of her dress went down to her hands, and she and Mrs. Washington looked almost like a queen and princess, sitting beside each other on the slightly raised platform.

"It is a pleasure to meet you, Mr. Revere. What were you discussing with the President?" Mrs. Adams asked suspiciously.

I thought of how to reply.

"Well?" Mrs. Adams asked, as everyone waited.

An artist's representation of one of Martha Washington's parties as first lady. Before there were state dinners, she called her gatherings levees.

"Leave this dear man alone," Mrs. Washington said with a smile. "He seems to have been made nervous by your teasing."

I fidgeted and took a deep breath. I did not know exactly what to say, but I wanted to make sure Cam had some more ideas for his playbook. "Mrs. Washington, my student here, Cam, is learning about the presidency and leadership. I am sorry to bother you, but would you mind sharing some characteristics of a good leader that President Washington possesses?"

Mrs. Adams was still staring at me as I stood with Cam beside me.

Mrs. Washington paused for a moment, "Not a bother at all, Mr. Revere and Cam. The qualities that come to mind are humility and dedication to family. But these things are seen from my perspective, which is limited."

I thought to myself that she was showing humility herself, as I knew she was very aware of the military and government. This piqued my interest so I asked, "Mrs. Washington, I read that you helped the soldiers during the awful winter at Valley Forge."

"Yes, you are correct, Mr. Revere," she replied, "but I was there merely to support my husband's effort. Those poor soldiers were cold and hungry and missed their families. All of them sacrificed dearly. I was happy to do a little in my own way to help. But as I said, I do not know of military affairs." She took a sip of tea.

At that moment, the President walked into the room and was immediately surrounded by guests. He looked unhappy. Mrs. Washington and Mrs. Adams stood, bowed, and politely excused themselves. They both walked over to the President. Mrs. Washington slid her arm under his and led him to a quieter corner to answer questions together.

I did not want to bother them so Cam and I exited through the swinging door at the side of the house.

"How are we going to find Liberty?" Cam asked.

"I'm not sure," I said. "He usually shows up when you need him."

Just then, Liberty backed out from behind the mansion.

"Liberty," I whispered, but loudly, "what are you doing?" We quickly walked over to meet him. Upon closer inspection, I noticed he had a large, thick piece of chalk in his mouth.

"You're just in time," Liberty mumbled, the chalk stick wiggling as he talked. "I was just admiring my work." He stepped back a few more feet from the back side of the brick mansion, staring in admiration.

I turned and nearly gasped in horror.

Liberty had drawn the words THE AMERICAN ADVEN-TURERS in fancy script letters. The words were part of a colorful collage of objects from our time-travel adventures—the *Mayflower* ship, an American flag, what looked to be a horse with a rider, possibly Paul Revere. On closer review, I noticed that the *Mayflower* had a pile of apples on the front bow.

Quietly, Liberty asked, "What do you think?"

What did I think? It was a beautiful, masterful work of . . . graffiti.

"Honestly, Liberty?" I said. "It's a masterpiece. But how do we explain how this got here on President Washington's house?"

"Just tell him your rebel horse did it. I'm sure he'll believe you," Cam snickered.

"Riiiiiight," I said.

Liberty shrugged. "Well, after waiting for you for like a million years, I remembered I had a package of sidewalk chalk in my

The Washington family sat for this portrait in the winter of 1789–1790 while they lived in New York. Do you recognize the children in this picture?

saddlebag. Now everyone will know that the American Adventurers were here!"

"We're supposed to be time-traveling in secret, remember?" I said.

"Oh, it'll wash off. No harm done," Liberty said.

I looked up and saw thick clouds above. *I hope it rains soon,* I thought.

"Now that our time-travel visit is over," said Cam, "can we *chalk it up* as a success?"

Both Cam and Liberty started laughing.

"Very funny," I said. "Seriously, let's time-jump out of this place before the colonial police arrest us."

And we did.

Chapter 5

The next morning, after a good night's sleep, we arrived early at Boston Bagels. Cam was already waiting for us, sitting in his mom's car in the parking lot. When he saw us he grabbed his backpack and got out of the car. He waved goodbye to his mom and she waved hello to us.

When Cam's mom drove away, he walked over and said, "I've got my Campaign Playbook, Mr. Revere, and I'm ready!"

When we found a table, Cam pulled his notebook out of his backpack. It had a George Washington picture on the cover and the title "Cam's Playbook."

Standing beside Liberty, I said, "I love it!"

We ordered breakfast and brought it back outside so we could eat with Liberty.

"Here you go, not one but three bagels to start your day,"

I said, cheerfully placing two garlic bagels and one onion bagel in front of Liberty.

"Whoa, this is my lucky day. Now we're talking," he said, before scooping up a bagel. "Thank you!" he mumbled between chews.

"I wish Nelly and Wash could be here. They were really fun," said Cam.

I took a sip of my coffee and agreed. "It was truly incredible to be right there with the Washingtons. I will never forget that visit."

"No way," Cam said, shaking his head, then flicking a stray sesame seed in the air.

"So here is another bit of strategy to add to your playbook," I said.

Cam turned to the first blank page after his current notes.

"You already completed two plays in the campaign. The first was to find out the rules of the election. The second was to decide for sure to run for president, and to sign up. You did both of those things, so I think you are ready for play three. The great part is that George and Martha Washington already gave you all you need and that is to understand what it means to be a good leader."

Cam wrote down, "Play three, *understand what it means to be a good leader.*"

"George Washington was an exceptional leader, who worked hard, overcame very challenging times, and served others. Both he and Mrs. Washington were also humble and focused on their family. And most important, he loved our country and tried to make the best decisions for the people."

Liberty looked around, perhaps hoping for another bagel, but surprisingly kept quiet.

"Presidents and leaders have to make a lot of decisions. You know what was one of President Washington's best decisions ever?" I asked.

Cam looked at me curiously but didn't reply.

"President Washington surrounded himself with a very solid team of trusted people. When he became president, he knew that unlike a king, he could not do the job alone. You can call that play four in your playbook: picking a good team."

Cam wrote down, "Play four, *pick a good team.*"

I added, "There was so much responsibility on his shoulders; one of his first tasks as president was to find dedicated people to share the burden."

"Oh, that is really smart. It is hard to do it on your own, especially against someone like Elizabeth," Liberty interjected. "Your campaign advisor agrees."

I smiled. "Washington recruited men like Thomas Jefferson, his secretary of state; Alexander Hamilton, his secretary of the Treasury; and, of course, you've met Henry Knox, his secretary of war. Oh, let's not forget James Madison, who helped President Washington set up a new federal government. These people were trusted friends, people he could count on."

Cam nodded, paying close attention.

The door behind us opened and closed as people hurried in and out, coffee and bagels in hand.

Liberty cleared his throat and said, "So, as your campaign advisor extraordinaire, I'm thinking you need a solid team. Team Cam. Cam's Team. President Cam's Team. Cam's Presidential Team. You know, any of those work."

"Okay, that makes sense to me," said Cam. "But who will be on

Alexander Hamilton served as the first secretary of the
Treasury in George Washington's cabinet along
with Thomas Jefferson and Henry Knox.

my team? I mean, I don't really know anyone who ran for president of anything before."

"That's okay," I replied. "Your team members don't really need a lot of experience on a presidential campaign. But they do need a desire to help you win and they need to be dedicated and trustworthy."

Cam scrunched his forehead.

Liberty said, "Remember GW's team was the first, too. They had no clue what to do, either."

"That's right, Liberty," I said. "They had to learn as they went."

Cam thought for a minute more before writing down another note. He leaned back in his chair and said, "I definitely need people on my team to help me win this. I mean, Elizabeth has like eight hundred cheerleaders and her dad is Principal Sherman."

Liberty interjected, "As your trusted campaign advisor, I highly recommend a young lady named Freedom. She is super-duper creative and could make ridiculously good signs for you. And we know she's really smart and definitely has your back."

I nodded and added, "I agree. Freedom is creative, smart, and hardworking. She gets along with just about everyone. And she has a lot of friends in the art program. They could help draw signs and get the word out to other students to vote for Cam."

"Did you say you agree with me?" Liberty asked. "I'm on a roll this morning. Ka-ching, deposit that into the Bank of Liberty Is Right."

We spent the next few minutes talking about other possible members of Cam's election team and how they could help. Just then, I felt a tap on my shoulder. I turned around to see Joseph standing behind me. "Good morning, everyone, how are we today?" he said, smiling widely.

"Good morning, sir," I replied. "We are doing quite well, and yourself?"

"Splendid," he replied, with joy visible on his mature face. "May I join you for a minute?" he asked.

"By all means," I said, standing up to pull out a spare chair.

He put his coffee on the table and said, "Ever since you told me young Cam here is running for student body president, I've been thinking about what tips an old goat like me could pass on to help you with your election."

Cam smiled politely and took a sip of his hot chocolate.

I suddenly noticed Liberty was no longer standing near our table. But I still smelled garlic and onions so I assumed he was hiding nearby.

"Cam, you remember this gentleman, right, from when you and your dad came in? He is a former congressman from our state and is an expert on election campaigns."

Cam perked up at the word *campaign*.

Joseph laughed and said, "I wouldn't call myself an expert per se, but elections really do fascinate me. In fact, with the national presidential election going on in our country right now, I have talk radio and the news on constantly. I like to really know and understand what each candidate plans to do as the leader of our country."

I nodded.

Joseph continued, "All across America right now, people like you and me are gathering at places like this bagel shop to talk about the election. They want to know as much as they can about the candidates in order to make an informed decision this November. It is these conversations and debates that most inspire me. What do you think, Cam?"

"Um, it seems like people are arguing a lot, too," Cam replied.

"Well, I guess you could think of it like that, but I prefer to think they are expressing their First Amendment right of free speech. In some other countries, people are afraid to discuss politics. But, anyway, enough about the national election. How is your campaign going?"

"Really well, thank you," Cam answered. He thumbed through the pages. "This is what I have so far: find out the rules, decide to run and sign up, understand what it means to be a good leader, and pick a good team. All those things are done, so we're now thinking of new plays to win."

Congressman Joseph clapped his hands and gave his wide smile.

Cam continued, "The only little problem is that there's this mean girl who is running against me named Elizabeth. She has lots of friends, but whatever."

Joseph nodded sincerely. "It doesn't seem like Elizabeth has the right mindset to be a good president, but it sounds like you have a good strategy for your campaign so far. My one small bit of advice to add to your plays is to not let anyone get you off your game. Don't worry about this Elizabeth girl having a lot of friends and fancy speeches. Don't change your campaign to copy hers. You cannot lead from the back. You and your team need to play harder, smarter, tougher. Use some elbow grease to drum up more votes."

"Thanks! What is elbow grease, Congressman?" Cam asked.

"Oh, you never heard that expression? It just means to work hard. Just outplay Elizabeth and you will get the votes to win."

"Thank you very much. Great advice, indeed," I said.

"Also, write down what you think are your strengths and weaknesses and those of your team," Joseph noted. "That way everyone can play their role most efficiently. You don't want two people doing the same thing at once, wasting precious time."

Cam nodded.

"Now that I am sure I bored you all, I'll leave you with that and let you get back to your day. Good luck, Cam campaign team," Joseph said as he politely got up from the table and headed toward his car.

"Thank you, Congressman Joseph," Cam said politely.

Liberty exhaled and materialized near our table. Cam and I gagged at the wave of garlic and onion breath.

"I knew you were still around, Liberty," I said. "Why did you turn invisible?"

"Sometimes I do my best thinking when I'm undercover," he replied. "Well, and because the Congressman may wonder what I'm doing here. I mean it is a breakfast table, not a barn, just sayin'. Even if I were a circus horse."

I laughed and said, "I think we are right on track. Congressman Joseph also stressed that we need a team." We all sat thinking for a few minutes without saying anything.

Cam tapped his hand on the tabletop and said, "Okay, okay, how about this? Freedom, Tommy, and Ed? I haven't seen Ed in a while but he was a big help to our dodgeball team—remember his sticky green suit? Ed knows a ton of people that Tommy and Freedom don't know. I mean he tutors half the school in math and he knows all the band kids."

"Perfect," I said, clapping my hands together. "President Washington would be very proud of you, Cam. You are really thinking through your team and how they can help you win your election. Superb. This is all part of creating a good election strategy."

Cam wrote notes in his playbook. I looked down at my watch and realized the school day was about to begin.

Cam thanked me for breakfast, grabbed his backpack, and ran off ahead with a big smile. Liberty and I followed to be sure he made it to school safely.

I thought, *Cam is so excited about this election and I am happy to encourage him, but what if it goes badly? What if Elizabeth beats him in a landslide? What then?*

I guess I must have been talking out loud because Liberty stopped, shook his head, and said, "Revere, you always say everything works out like it's supposed to. You have to work hard for what you want even if it ends badly at first. If you're gonna quit you may as well sit."

I nodded and said, "Yes, that does sound a bit like me. You are right, Liberty."

I noticed his eyes widen and mouth begin to open, so I jumped in. "Wait, I'll say it for you. Deposit that into the Bank of Liberty Was Right."

Liberty nodded deeply and smiled triumphantly.

"Oh, yeah, and we definitely need to stop off and get you some breath mints before the Environmental Protection Agency fines us for releasing harmful amounts of garlic and onions into the air," I said, laughing.

We arrived at Manchester Middle School just as classes were ending. I left Liberty outside and headed into our American Adventurers club classroom.

Before I could even put my bag down, Freedom came running up to my desk and said excitedly, "I'm in. I can totally help Cam. Elizabeth isn't nice and she shouldn't be president. She has posters up all around school. They are pink and sparkly, yuck. I'm going to design some for Cam."

"I am glad you are on Cam's team, Freedom. I know you will help."

Freedom nodded and went back to her seat, just as Cam bounded into the classroom. He came straight to my desk and said, breathing heavily, "Mr. Revere, what do you think about flyers? I mean, Freedom can't really draw a bunch of signs quickly. My mom volunteers at the library and could totally make copies on the copy machine for us once Freedom creates them. That way we would have more to hand out and put up around school."

"I love that idea," I said, proud of Cam's strategic thinking. "You are on a roll, and Freedom told me she is already on board. We just need to double-check the election rules on how many flyers you can hand out, et cetera."

Cam nodded and said, "Okay. Everyone is in, even Ed. He said he'd spread the word during band practice, and maybe come up with a great campaign song. By the way, where's Tommy?"

"Right here!" Tommy answered. He walked into the room with a big smile and said, "I'm not late, am I? I was talking to some of the football guys about your campaign. I recruited a few volunteers to help us. They think we need T-shirts like Elizabeth has, but with much more school spirit."

Cam high-fived Tommy. "Awesome. Thanks," he said. "Maybe they can help out with the shirts."

"This is all a good play to add to your playbook," I said. "How about we call it play five: Communication Strategy with the Students. It can cover the flyers, shirts, posters, and every other way you play to get your message out."

Cam agreed and wrote down the play and other ideas.

When the rest of the students entered the classroom we played a little game based on the national presidential election.

I divided the class in half and explained that today's game was called Hot Seat. I held up an example photo and said, "Okay, team Red and team Blue, here in my fingers, I hold a picture of a famous place in America."

The class strained to look carefully from their seats.

"I have a stack on my desk of ten famous American people, places, and things. Each round you will nominate one of your team to sit in the hot seat here at the front of the class. I will hold up a picture and show both team members in the hot seat. The student who rings and guesses who or what the picture is correctly wins that round. The team with the most points gets a free ice cream sundae coupon, and, of course, bragging rights!"

The class smiled.

"That's fun. It's like hot potato, kind of," said the girl sitting next to Freedom.

"Easy peasy, got this one easy, Mr. Revere," Tommy announced, clapping his hands.

"Keep in mind, only your team members can sit in the hot seat. So just like in baseball, pick your hot-seat lineup carefully. The questions may or may not get harder." I winked.

I pulled two chairs side by side at the front of the room. "All right, here we go. Red team and Blue team, send up your first hot-seat player."

Tommy raced to the hot seat, followed closely by a dark-haired boy from the back of the room.

"Are you ready? Steady? Okay, question one: What is this item, and what historical figure is pictured in the center?" I quickly flashed a picture of a one-dollar bill.

Tommy rang a fake buzzer with his thumb first and shouted, "Got it!"

I nodded for him to go ahead. "That, my friends, is a one-dollar bill with our first president, George Washington." Tommy jumped out of his seat, pretending to put out the flames under him. He bowed to the crowd, smiling widely.

The students clapped and laughed as their teams rang in with answers.

"Anyway, that's all for today, everyone," I said, closing the club for the day.

As the classroom emptied, Cam, Tommy, and Freedom lagged behind to walk out with me.

Tommy gave a thumbs-up and said, "Great meeting, Mr. Revere. I didn't think I would really like after-school anything, besides football, but this club is actually really fun."

I smiled and said with a wink, "That's great. I told you American politics is hip."

"Oh, yeah, Mr. Revere, it's super-hip," Freedom said with a smile and sideways glance.

Cam smiled too, then turned to me and said, "Mr. Revere, the three of us were brainstorming at lunch and came up with a new campaign saying. Wanna hear it?"

"I think you mean a slogan? Sure, I'd love to," I replied as we exited the front of the school and headed toward the oak tree where I hoped to find Liberty.

Cam grinned and said, "'Pump up the Jam—Vote for Cam for Student Body President.'" Cam flicked up the collar on his shirt and spun around with flair.

Freedom looked at me and asked, "What do you think?"

I smiled. "Well, it's catchy . . . and it's even choreographed with a dance move. Maybe Ed's band can help out with a hip tune?"

All three of them rolled their eyes playfully.

Freedom added, "Okay, maybe we should work on it a bit more."

When we reached the oak tree, Cam looked around and asked, "Where's Liberty? I thought he was my campaign advisor."

I looked in all directions but didn't see him.

"There he is," Freedom said, pointing straight behind me. I looked over my shoulder to see Liberty's mane flopping in the wind as he raced toward us. He was panting when he arrived.

"Gee, Liberty, so glad you could join us," I said. "Dare I ask where you were?"

Liberty said between breaths, "As a matter of fact . . . I have been very . . . very busy . . . top secret . . . important campaign business."

I gave him a skeptical look.

Liberty took a long breath and exhaled. He replied, "While you guys were in your American Adventurers club meeting, I went to go nibble some grass. You know, just doing my part to keep the lawn looking good. When all of a sudden I saw them."

"Saw who?" Tommy asked, putting his thumbs under the straps of his backpack.

"Elizabeth! And her minions," Liberty exclaimed.

"Ugh, man. Eliza-brat strikes again," Cam said, sighing.

Liberty rolled his eyes. "I know, right. Elizabeth was standing in front of a bunch of girls on the football field, maybe boys, too, I don't know. She was talking about something and all these kids started laughing hysterically at the same time. I thought it was very suspicious, so I hustled back here to report."

Cam looked like he wanted to punch something. "Ugh," he said.

Freedom's eyes darted back and forth between Cam and me, nervously.

Tommy interjected, "Are they still there?"

Still wide-eyed, Liberty replied, "I'm not sure, but I'm pretty sure I heard Cam's name. Or maybe they were talking about cans of yam or jam in a can or maybe there was a scam between a ham and some Spam."

I held up one hand to stop Liberty's stream of consciousness and said, "Hey, guys, let's not worry about what Elizabeth is doing. Let's focus on our plan and Cam's next steps. We have plenty—" Before I could finish, Cam started running toward the fields.

"Come on, let's go find out!" Cam yelled back at us.

Freedom shrugged her shoulders and took off running after Cam. Tommy sprinted after Freedom.

Liberty gave me a glance and said, "Um, I'm thinking they aren't buyin' the whole *let's focus on Cam's plan* thing."

Ignoring Liberty, I sucked in a large breath and said, "Let's go see where they're going." We followed the rest of the crew.

When we got to the edge of the field, sure enough, Elizabeth and a large group of cheerleaders were huddled around a bench on the sideline. There were some athletic boys standing nearby. It looked like a pregame warm-up meeting.

Liberty sighed and said, "See, I told you."

"What is she doing? I can't hear what they are talking about from here," Cam said. He was clearly frustrated.

"Yeah, what is she saying?" Tommy asked, straining to hear.

Liberty took a deep breath and went into stealth mode. After waiting for thirty seconds or so, he reappeared. He looked almost scared.

"What is she saying?" asked Cam.

"Do I have to tell you?" Liberty hesitated.

"Yes, all of it," Cam demanded.

"I'm not so sure. But I think she said she's going to destroy you and embarrass you, and make you cry," Liberty replied.

"Are you sure about that?" I asked. "Maybe you misunderstood."

Cam hit his hand into his fist and said forcefully, "She's not going to destroy me. And she's definitely not going to make me cry." His face was getting redder.

"I really don't like her," Freedom said, shaking her head.

In the distance we could see the group laughing, clapping, and hollering like they were at a pep rally.

"Why is she so popular? She's so mean," Freedom said, frowning.

Cam yelled, "That's it, I'm done!" He started charging toward Elizabeth's campaign rally. "Embarrass me? Are you kidding?" With each word he sounded angrier and angrier.

"Cam, come back!" Freedom shouted.

Just then, Tommy ran after Cam and quickly caught up to him. Whatever he said was enough to make Cam turn around and start walking back toward us.

I tugged Liberty's bridle and said, "Come on, guys, let's go. Follow me."

Freedom turned to follow Liberty.

Tommy pulled Cam by the shirt and they both followed silently.

When we got closer to the classroom, I tried to calm the situation down. I said, "All right, that wasn't the best—"

Cam interrupted. "Wasn't the best? She just insulted me in front of everyone. They all laughed at me." He sighed and tilted back his head, clearly exasperated. Cam was obviously in no mood to talk about our team election strategy.

Liberty piped up. "Elizabeth can say whatever she wants. Sticks and stones, Cam. But we know you're the man. You're Super Cam."

Freedom nodded and added, "She's just scared you're going to win, so she's being extra mean."

I patted Cam on the back and asked him to take a little walk with me. After he had cooled down a bit, I suggested we all meet in the morning at our campaign headquarters. Everything always looks better in the morning. I filled Freedom and Tommy in on our breakfast routine and said I would coordinate with them a little later.

Things did look better the next morning, and we continued to meet before school every day to discuss the progress of the campaign.

Around a week later, on our way to Boston Bagels to meet the crew, Liberty grinned from ear to ear. He sang "Buh-buh-buh-bagel time" the entire way. Just after we arrived, Cam, Tommy, and Freedom were dropped off by their families.

We sat at our regular table, which was fully stocked with breakfast sandwiches and hot drinks. In between bites, Liberty made jokes, stopping only when a customer passed by. "Boston Bagels are the most de-li-cious and nutritious. Best bagels any-where, hooves down." He smiled, contently.

"I love this cinnamon raisin bagel," Freedom said, wiping her chin politely with her napkin.

Tommy nodded. "Totally," he said. He placed his hand on Cam's shoulder.

Cam still looked annoyed. He had hardly touched his breakfast.

I knew I had to turn this ship around and quickly. "Okay, let's review," I said. "If my memory serves correctly, Candidate Cam has five campaign plays in effect right now: he learned the rules, signed up to run, understands what it means to be a good leader, established a team, and came up with a communication strategy, including a slogan in the works. He also gathered advice from Congressman Joseph, and met George and Martha Washington for inside information."

"What an awesome start," Freedom said sweetly.

"Now, you've got about two weeks until the big election and vote, and I think you are doing great so far. But there is more to learn and more work to do so you can win!" I said.

Cam sighed and didn't comment.

"Seriously, man, you totally got this," Tommy said in encouragement.

"I don't even know what I'm running for. I thought I was going to be cool and win this easily and now Elizabeth is totally taking over everything. She's got posters everywhere, the whole school probably knows by now that she's running, and her stuff is all perfect," Cam said, looking down at the table.

"Cam, remember what both George Washington and Congressman Joseph said. There are going to be many tough days, but you have to rise above them like a strong leader and don't let anything rattle you," I said. "And remember, the American Patriots were always the underdogs. No one ever thought they would beat the huge British superpower."

"But we did!" Tommy shouted.

Cam raised his eyebrows and nodded but did not comment.

I nodded and agreed. "Yes, because of the work of great leaders like George Washington, who never gave up and who led the Patriots even when they were totally discouraged."

"I get it, Mr. Revere," Cam said, but he was looking down at the table.

Liberty swallowed the bagel he was chewing, licked his lips, and said, "I agree with Revere. Don't sweat this stuff, Cam my man; turn the pain into gain, don't let little Lizzy rain on your parade."

I looked over at Liberty with one eyebrow raised.

We all looked at each other without saying anything. Freedom was nervously fidgeting with her wrapper.

I didn't think I was making any headway when the silence broke.

Cam clapped his hands together once like a coach and said, "Okay, I'm shaking it off." He held his arms out in front of him and did a little shake. He added, "I'm back. We are going to win this. Elizabeth, bring it on!" His eyes narrowed.

Freedom smiled and cheered, "All right, Cam!"

Tommy gave Cam a high five, Cam gave Freedom a high five, Freedom gave Liberty a high five, and Liberty tried to give me a high hoof.

When Cam was "on" he could capture a room. He had a presence about him like any great leader.

"Come on, everybody; you too, Liberty—huddle up," Cam said. We put our hands and a hoof together and said in unison, "One, two, three, Team Cam!"

The alarm on my digital watch started to buzz. It was time to make our way to school before the first bell. Cam was pumped up again and seemed back in the game.

As we all approached Manchester Middle, I felt the morning campaign meeting was a success after all. Cam was walking confidently with his head held up high and laughing at Tommy's jokes. We were making our way toward the front of the school, when an all-too-familiar voice shouted, "Hey, nerds!"

I froze for a second.

Sure enough, Elizabeth and a group of cheerleaders were standing by the flagpole, scowling. Cam looked at Elizabeth with a serious stare.

I took a deep breath and tried to think of something to say.

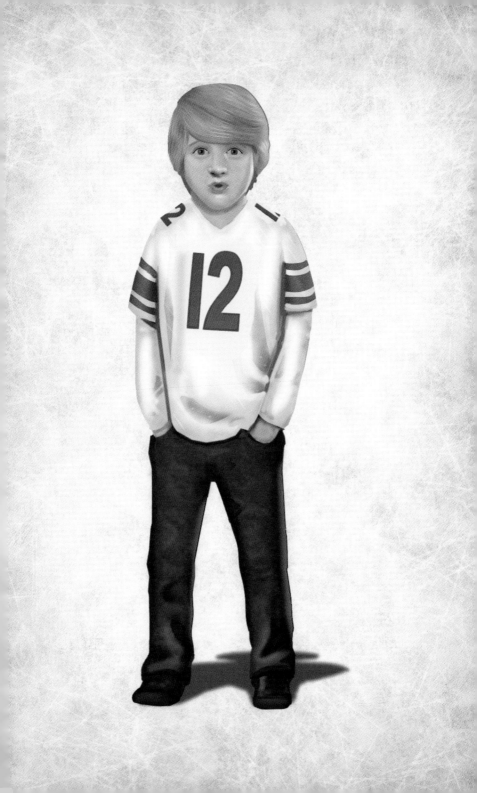

Chapter 6

*T*hat afternoon, the American Adventurers were full of energy. Principal Sherman made it very clear that our club could not play any more dunk tank games, but surprisingly he forgot to mention anything about a horse on school grounds. Nonetheless, I asked Liberty to keep a low profile.

Liberty stood outside the classroom's open window, facing a paper airplane that lay on the windowsill. The nose of the plane tilted upward. Written on both sides of the plane in black marker were the words AIR FORCE ONE. It was a mini version of the President's plane.

"Is everybody ready?" I asked.

The students all nodded.

Liberty's wild, unbridled imagination had done it again by inventing a game he called Catch and Answer.

"This is our final round," I said. "I didn't realize the time was so late."

"I'm catching this one, Mr. Revere," Cam said.

"Not if I can help it," said Tommy, grinning.

Other club members joined in. "Air Force One is coming to me," said a girl with pink glasses.

Even Freedom was getting into it. "You boys are going down," she teased.

I laughed. "All right, Liberty, on the count of three," I said. "One, two, three!"

Liberty put his mouth near the back of the paper airplane and took a deep breath. When he exhaled sharply, the plane shot off the windowsill and launched into the air. Needless to say, my new students were impressed with my *trained* horse. *If they only knew*, I thought.

In the final round, the plane went high and did a loop-the-loop. Hands and arms were stretched out, trying to catch Air Force One. It dipped sharply, zipped by several students, and headed straight for Freedom. At the last second, Tommy poked her gently in the ribs. She instinctively tucked her arms in while Cam snatched the plane from the air.

"No fair," said Freedom, crossing her arms.

Cam held the paper airplane in his hand and raced around the room, yelling, "President Cam takes off in his Air Force One!" When he passed by the open window he patted Liberty on the nose, laughing.

"Catch and answer, Cam," I said. "You caught the plane so now you have to answer one of these two questions to win."

"No problem, Mr. Revere, I'm ready," he said.

"I like your confidence. The first question is: Lots of people on TV and radio are talking about the current president of the United States coming to the end of the term. What is a *term of office?*"

Cam thought for a few seconds, then said, "Is it when the president is talking and it's the word at the end of the speech?"

"Good guess," I said, "but in this case *term* refers to the length of time the president holds the position. President Washington resigned after two terms. Most presidents only are elected to one term, but President Franklin Delano Roosevelt was elected to four terms. After his presidency, the Congress passed the Twenty-Second Amendment to the Constitution. Now a president can only serve two terms. Your second question is: How long is a presidential term?"

"Oh, I got this one Mr. Revere. Four years!"

"Well done, Cam," I said, applauding, along with the students.

Just then an idea popped into my head. "You know, Cam, there's just a couple of minutes left, enough time for you to tell the class what you promise to do as the new student body president."

"You mean, give a speech? Now?" Cam asked, as he returned to his seat.

"Yes, just a practice speech to help other students know why they should vote for you."

"Okay, um, sure," replied Cam, hesitantly. He grabbed his playbook from his desk. Every time I saw him in the last few days, he had his head in the playbook, either taking notes or studying. I was sure he knew the plans and ideas backward to forward. All he needed to do was add a dash of his charming charisma to the speech and it would be wonderful. I was excited to hear how he would present his strategy.

He stood up and walked to the front of the class. When he turned around, all of the students were looking directly at him. Instead of launching into his speech with gusto, as I thought he

George Washington served two terms as the first president
of the United States from April 30, 1789, until December 14, 1797.
Why was George Washington a great leader?

would, Cam looked as though he was trying to say something but the words were not coming out. He began to fidget with his pockets. He looked down at his playbook as if he was searching for something, and flipped through the pages.

"Go ahead, Cam," I said, encouragingly.

"I want to be student . . . um, yah, so. I uh . . ." His face was turning red and I could see his hand begin to tremble.

Freedom looked back at me with a nervous look.

Tommy sat up straight and said, "Go on, Cam, you are awesome, man." I could tell he was worried about his friend.

The seconds ticked past, and then a minute, but Cam had still not said anything. He stood motionless at the front of the class, looking down at his playbook.

Suddenly, the classroom door swung open. I almost couldn't believe my eyes. Elizabeth came breezing into the classroom like a windstorm, one hand on her hip.

"Oh wow, looks like Cam's going to give a speech. Let's hear it." She walked over to the nearest desk and sat down. "Go ahead, Cam, don't let me bother you." She flicked her long blond hair to one side.

"Hello, Elizabeth, thank you for joining us. Please remain quiet while in the club meeting," I said.

Elizabeth pursed her lips and sat up straight, looking forward. Out of the corner of my eye, I saw Liberty duck away from the window.

"Were you spying on us through the door?" asked Freedom, who was sitting two desks away from Elizabeth.

Elizabeth turned in her seat and stared at Freedom, but didn't respond.

"What's wrong, Cam, can't you think of anything to say?" said Elizabeth.

Cam's eyes were open wide in shock.

Tommy glanced back at me and shrugged.

The other students started to grab their backpacks.

Freedom looked kindly at Cam, urging him to continue, but he stood frozen.

Another few seconds passed, as Cam tried to speak: "No, Elizabeth, um, I am good to be . . . president . . . uh, I'm a leader . . . um, fun . . ." Then he went silent again.

Before I could put a stop to it, Elizabeth broke the silence and said, "Well, I *always* have something to say." She stood from her seat and walked to the front of the class. She was wearing skinny jeans, high-top trendy pink sneakers with glitter, and a T-shirt that read QUEEN E. The new club members watched with backpacks in hand while Cam sheepishly moved off to the side.

"If you want to be cool in school, vote for me, Elizabeth, for student body president. When I run, I'll make it fun. You'll see." Her words flowed out flawlessly. She waved like she was on a tour bus and captivated the entire room. Then she slipped out of the room as quickly as she had appeared.

Almost everyone clapped.

Cam's mouth dropped open.

Just when I thought the threat was gone, Elizabeth popped her head into the classroom again and said, "Oh, and by the way Cam, great speech. You have *such* a way with words." She giggled as she bowed back out into the hall, waving at everyone like a princess. I could hear other girls laughing outside, too.

"Our club is dismissed," I said.

Everyone but Cam, Tommy, and Freedom left to head home.

Cam's face was red and he looked angry, still standing at the front of the room.

My stomach was in knots. The idea to have Cam practice his speech was a complete disaster.

"Let's meet Liberty outside by the big oak tree," I said.

We silently exited the school. When we reached the oak, Cam threw his backpack against the tree and slumped to the ground.

"Gather around," I said. "Remember how George Washington always remained cool under pressure?" I paused, looking everyone in the eye. "Elizabeth knows how to apply pressure. But when fighting the British superpower, the American Patriots didn't give up, did they? And neither will Cam."

Cam did not say anything and just sat with his jaw clenched and arms crossed. The sky above the tree was mostly blue, but an area of clouds in the distance made houses on the horizon appear foggy.

Freedom said, "C'mon, Cam, cheer up, it's going to be okay."

"I should be the only one with the long face," Liberty snorted, laughing at his own joke. Then he moved his nose left and right to emphasize the punch line. He looked disappointed when no one immediately laughed.

Eventually Tommy smiled but Cam's unhappy expression did not change. "I'm sorry I let you down in there, Mr. Revere. I looked like such an idiot," he said.

"No, no, you did *not* let me down, Cam. If anything, I'm the one to blame for setting you up. But, no matter, I have a plan." We all had unconsciously formed a circle around Cam.

"He's always the man with the plan," said Liberty, nodding.

"Okay, so here it is," I said. "You think George Washington is pretty amazing, right? How about we go back and talk to President Washington a little more about how he remains calm under pressure? We've learned so many great tips from him already, it could only help your campaign."

Cam shrugged his shoulders.

"Wait, I've got it, even better," I said. "As we had a bit of a hiccup in the speech department, let's focus our strategy on great speeches under pressure. I think we should visit President Washington near the end of his second term in office in 1797. That's when he gave his greatest speech of all time to the American people."

Freedom's hand shot up. "I wanna go!" she exclaimed.

"Bummer. I wish I could go," Tommy said, "but I have a game coming up and my coach said that trampolines, skateboards, and horses are off-limits. He didn't say anything about time portals, but . . ."

"No worries, Tommy," I said. "Next time."

"Speaking of my coach, I'm late for practice. See you tomorrow." He darted across the grass.

"Okay, let's do it, Mr. Revere," said Cam. "I think it will pump me up to see George Washington's speech." He looked like he was struggling to find any kind of excitement.

I handed Freedom and Cam their colonial outfits, which they slipped over their regular clothes. Then they climbed up onto Liberty.

When everyone was ready, Liberty looked both ways to make sure we were alone, and said, "*Rush, rush, rushing to history!*"

A sparkling orb appeared out of nowhere and expanded to the size of a giant boulder.

As Liberty ran to jump into the swirling yellow and purple

sphere, I said, "March 4, 1797, George Washington, the President's House, Philadelphia."

We landed near a large tree canopy behind a wall and an iron gate. A bright red cardinal flew past us and over a fountain at the center of a small green park. I looked up to see the side of a three-story building, with another similar-sized building attached. It was early in the morning and the streets were quiet. It was neither cloudy nor sunny, and a light breeze pushed through the air.

"Here we are," I said. "Follow me."

Cam and Freedom dismounted from Liberty and we walked through the open gate. On our left was a mansion. It looked like a large house of today, with formal windows and brick walls overlooking a busy street.

"Wow, that is a really pretty house," Freedom said, looking up.

"It is the President's House," I said, feeling warmth in my chest at the history in front of us. "Remember that President Washington lived here in Philadelphia, the temporary capital until Washington, D.C., was finalized."

"I am glad your trip here was enjoyable," Liberty interjected. "I do accept time-travel tips."

Freedom laughed and patted Liberty on his side. Then she gave him a crisp carrot from his saddlebag. Both she and Cam looked the part, with her long hair tucked in a bonnet, and his white collared shirt covered in a jacket. They looked like characters in an old painting.

"Are Nelly and Wash here?" Cam asked. "Maybe we can hang out?"

I nodded. "I bet they are, but remember, this is seven years

You can see this statue of George Washington on horseback
in the Boston Public Garden in Massachusetts.
George Washington is considered by many to be our greatest president.

after we last visited the family. I might be able to get away with it, but they may wonder how you are still the same age."

Cam snapped his fingers and said, "I'll just say I am his younger brother and we look a lot alike."

Liberty shook his body giggling and added, "Some would say you look like identical twins, wink-wink."

"Oh, I always wanted a twin," said Freedom.

It was nice to see Cam's mood improve. "So how are we gonna get in there?" he asked. "It doesn't look like they are having a party this time." He strained to look through the tall windows of the President's House.

Liberty stood absentmindedly chewing on the carrot tip like a cow in a pasture and said, "How about you just tell them we're here to hang out with the President?"

I looked at him with an eyebrow raised. "That is certainly getting right to the point, but we may need to come up with a better excuse."

Liberty shrugged his shoulders. "I might be able to come up with one if I had another carrot. Chewing always makes me think better."

Freedom snickered and grabbed a couple more carrots.

Cam looked at me quizzically. "Wait, why are we at the President's House, anyway? I thought you said he was giving an awesome speech to a big crowd of fans," he said. "I don't see any crowds around here. It's pretty quiet."

"I'm with Cam," Freedom added.

"Yes, I did say there would be a speech, but this speech was not actually given in front of crowds like his Inaugural Address," I said.

Cam's shoulders sank and he said, "Aw, man. That's the good part!"

I pulled out several papers that were neatly folded in my coat pocket. I held them up and said, "This speech was actually printed in the newspapers for masses of people to *read*. The speech is known as President Washington's Farewell Address. He worked on the incredibly important words, right here, at this house."

Cam scratched his head and asked, "Wait a minute—Farewell Address? Isn't *farewell* like goodbye? Why's he saying goodbye? Where's he going?"

"He is saying goodbye to the country by stepping down as president. This Farewell Address is both a goodbye and a warning to the American people," I replied.

"Wait, why? I don't get it. That is so dumb," Cam said. He shook his head. "I do not get this at all. Do people think he's doing a bad job? Did he freeze during a speech?" Cam was obviously still thinking about the incident in class earlier.

"Actually, no, just the opposite," I replied. "President Washington was doing a brilliant job as the first president. Almost everyone in the country had admiration and respect for him and wanted him to stay. In fact, many on his team begged him to continue. But George Washington thought the best decision was to step down."

"But why?" Cam argued. "It doesn't make any sense that he's leaving the coolest job ever. What am I missing? I thought you said he didn't quit anything. Now I need help on my election campaign and I can't even go to him anymore." Cam crossed his arms and stood in place.

"He is not quitting, Cam. By deciding to leave the presidency, at this moment in time, George Washington makes the United States of America stronger."

"Whatever," Cam said. "I still don't get it." He looked around as if he were searching for a better answer. "He had it all together, and then leaves—for what?"

At that moment, I understood. Cam was hoping to speak with his hero George Washington and forget the embarrassment of his encounter with Elizabeth. Now, to hear that the President left office, he was fighting his own battle not to quit.

Softly I said, "Think about it this way. Even the best baseball players have to eventually retire from the game. Not because they don't want the team to win anymore but because they know they need to make room for younger players to come in and learn. It is ultimately better for the team, long term."

Freedom said sympathetically, "So maybe President Washington wants to teach a younger president to be president."

I nodded. "Yes, in a way, Freedom. Essentially, if President Washington stayed on for life, he would become the king of America."

"Oh no, that's what Elizabeth wants to be at Manchester Middle School," Freedom said, with a sour look.

"President Washington did not want to be king," I said. "But nothing in the Constitution said he had to step down. By leaving on his own, he opened the process for the next election. People could vote for a new president."

Cam sighed. "I know, but *why?*"

I smiled. "Because he wanted to teach Americans that the presidency is more important than any one person. It was one of the greatest decisions in the history of the world."

Cam looked unsure but said, "Okay, I think I understand."

I smiled and patted him on the shoulder. A carriage passed behind us, and Liberty moved out of the way. Liberty looked

around for more carriages and then back toward the President's House. I followed his gaze.

"Look, there he is!" Liberty announced, out of the blue. Entirely distracted by the discussion, we had nearly missed President Washington walking right out the front door. "He's a little older, but it's definitely George Washington."

Two men bowed as they passed the President on the sidewalk.

"Where's he going?" Freedom asked.

"Yeah, what's he up to?" Cam added.

"Quickly. Let's follow him and find out," I replied. We rushed to catch up. I could not believe a president was walking by himself in public. That would never happen in modern day.

"Go faster, Mr. Revere. Maybe you can say hi," Freedom said, breathing a little heavier.

I wasn't sure this was the best idea. What would I say we were doing there?

"Go on, Revere," Liberty nudged.

I picked up my pace and hesitantly called out, "President Washington?"

He continued walking, looking straight ahead.

I remembered he didn't have the best hearing, which became an obstacle later in life. "President Washington?" I said in a louder voice, a few steps closer. The crew was sneaking along behind me.

"Good morning," he said in a straight tone and kept walking. He did not look directly at me and seemed focused. Lamplights were still flickering, as the sun was not fully up. Washington's powdered hair was pulled in a tight clip with a black bow on the end. He wore stockings, perfectly tidy shoes, and a velvet suit. The stoop in his broad shoulders was more pronounced, and although he still walked with a straight back, it seemed harder for him to move with grace.

Merchants, setting up their carts for the day, bowed deeply to him as he passed.

We followed closely, and I thought of ways to break the ice and remind him who I was. I did not want to miss our chance. After a block he turned and then turned again. He continued walking toward a building that resembled a stable. I could smell horses, leather, and hay as we approached, and could hear neighs and whinnies.

Cam and Freedom caught up with me but I noticed Liberty had disappeared.

As George Washington turned to walk into the stable, the sunlight reflected off a metal sword he wore at his waist.

I paused by the front entrance and whispered, "Let's follow him inside. But be careful, I'm not sure the President wants visitors right now."

"No problem, Mr. Revere," Cam said. "We can be stealthy like Liberty. Wait, where is Liberty?" he said, turning around.

"He says he's securing the perimeter like the Secret Service," Freedom said, smiling.

"Can't worry about Liberty right now," I replied. "Let's go."

As we slipped inside the stable, it took a few seconds for my eyes to adjust to the darkness. It was like walking into a movie theater before the show started. Cam and Freedom went to hide on a pile of hay in the back corner. I put my finger to my mouth and motioned for them to stay as quiet as possible.

Soon, I noticed George Washington standing beside a white horse, patting its nose. The President's head was tilted to one side and he wore a slight smile. There were other horses lined up in dark brown rooms floored with hay. Saddles and riding equipment hung on the walls and from the ceiling.

"Mr. President?" I asked, politely.

George Washington turned and waved me over. "Yes, sir. Please come closer. I forgot my glasses and am having trouble seeing you clearly," he said. His voice was low and scratchy. He looked much older than just seven years before. Despite being only around sixty-five years old, the decades on the battlefield and the pressure of being the leader of a new country had clearly affected him.

"It is me, Rush Revere, sir. We have met a few times over the years. I have not visited in some time."

President Washington paused for a moment and replied, "My apologies, Mr. Revere." He smiled gently. "My eyes have grown tired in service to our country."

Admiration swelled in my chest and I replied softly, "Yes, sir, I understand."

President Washington nodded and looked toward the white horse. "I'm afraid you've caught me in a pensive moment. I often come here for a quiet break from the noise. Today is quite an emotional day. These horses remind me of Mount Vernon. That is my home, my farm, the place of my family and their future, and where I will go to rest the remainder of my days."

As he said these words, President Washington's eyes transformed from stern to tender. Through the lamplight of the stable I noticed deep wrinkles etched on his face. His penetrating blue-gray eyes had developed a new softness over time. Each movement of his body seemed to cause pain. Still, his grace and dignity remained.

"I am sorry, sir, I do not want to interrupt your thoughts," I began. George Washington looked kindly toward me, placed a large, powerful hand on a nearby saddle, and let it rest tenderly. I continued, "You deserve to have peace and quiet after your decades of service to our country."

I slowly turned to walk out, to let him have his time alone.

"Mr. Revere," the President said with a strained voice. "It has taken me a moment to recall your last visit, but now I remember." He leaned over gingerly and pulled out two wooden stools, motioning for me to sit. "Now, we last met at the Cherry Street Mansion, correct? We went outside to get some air and Wash and Nelly played with one of your students."

"Yes, that is correct," I said softly, with my hands crossed on my knees. I sat beside the President quietly as sunlight began to stream in long, warm lines through slats in the windows. He looked at the horses and seemed to breathe the scene in. The room was remarkably quiet compared to the roaring packed streets of his inauguration eight years before.

As we listened to the horses eat hay or nicker in their stalls, I pulled the printed copy of his Farewell Address from my coat pocket and looked down at the beautiful words. It began:

Friends and Fellow Citizens: The period for a new election of a citizen to administer the executive government of the United States being not far distant . . .

"What are you reading, Mr. Revere?" the President asked.

"This is a copy of your address to the people, sir. I kept it from the newspaper." I knew with these words, George Washington was sharing his wisdom with the people, but I was eager to hear directly why he wrote them. "I told my students about the importance of this address to our country."

Friends and Fellow Citizens,

The period for a new election of a citizen to administer the executive government of the United States being not far distant, and the time actually arrived when your thoughts must be employed in designating the person who is to be clothed with that important trust, it appears to me proper, especially as it may conduce to a more distinct expression of the public voice, that I should now apprise you of the resolution I have formed, to decline being considered among the number of those out of whom a choice is to be made.

G. Washington

This is a section of George Washington's Farewell Address, one of the most important documents in American history. Do you know what the words mean?

I hoped Cam and Freedom were listening carefully.

President Washington looked down at the floor and said, "Thank you, Mr. Revere. I am happy to report that today I will retire from public office. The next president of the United States, John Adams, will be inaugurated not far from here."

March 4, 1797, was an important date in American history. It was the day George Washington peacefully transferred power to the next president. At the end of that day, the newly elected John Adams would take over. This had never happened before in history.

"Mr. President, my students have been asking me repeatedly if anyone asked you to stay on as president. Has anyone begged you to stay on for the good of the country?" I asked.

I feared the President might become upset. Instead, he simply stretched out a leg in front of him, looked over at me patiently, and said, "When Alexander Hamilton helped me to write this address to the people, he consistently urged me to continue as president. But it is time to resign."

I looked at the President with the purest admiration. I wanted to say that without his leadership the country might not have survived, and how much of an American hero he was.

The President continued, "But leaving is not without hesitation. Although I am eager to return home, I feel a deep sense of gratitude to my beloved country for the steadfast confidence and many honors it has given me. In reviewing the years of my presidential administration, I have not found intentional errors, but it is probable that I have committed many. I fervently hope that Almighty God will limit the bad effects of my mistakes, and that the country will understand why I made the decisions I did over forty-five years of public service."

I was mesmerized hearing the very sentiment of President Washington's Farewell Address repeated in person. I reminded myself to explain to the crew that he was grateful to the country and that he hoped the people would understand why he made the decisions he made.

The President added, "It was always the work of the people, not me; of the soldiers, and families who gave everything to the cause. The temporary value of my services to the country compare only in a tiny way to the work of the people."

I hoped Cam would remember all of this to write it down later in his playbook.

"Sir, if I were to tell my students your main reasons for writing this address and stepping down from your presidency, what would they be?"

The President thought for a moment and replied, "It is a goodbye and a warning. Tell your students to remember two things: One, we need a strong government to keep our freedoms and never to return to control by a king. Second, we cannot break into *factions*, or groups of people looking out for only themselves instead of the country."

"When you say factions, do you mean political parties?" I asked.

"In part, yes, but also divides between North and South. I feel this will eventually be negative for the country."

I was about to ask another question, but the President slowly rose to his feet. "Mr. Revere, it is time for us to part ways. It has been a pleasure speaking with you. I will leave you with this final thought for your students. The Constitution is only nine years old, so the people have not yet learned to fully embrace it. Your students must learn about the Constitution and the government, so we may remain *We the People*."

I bowed deeply to President Washington, and he turned. Cam and Freedom leaned back to hide as he gracefully exited the stable.

Gathering them, I said, "You guys listened so well. I am really proud of you."

"It's so sad he's leaving," Freedom said, visibly upset. She took one last look back at the horses.

At first Cam did not say anything and his face was somber. He was looking down the path where the President had just walked, as it wove and turned and finally intersected with the street. I regretted bringing him on this time-travel adventure. It had not given him the boost I had hoped for.

Then, to my surprise, out of the blue, Cam said, "It's like when my dad leaves for the military. He knows he has to go for the country, but he wants to stay with us, too."

I nodded and said, "That is an outstanding observation, Cam."

"Mr. Revere, I don't want to be cool anymore," Cam said. "I mean, I don't want to become president to be cool or popular. Before today, I thought being president was about all the crowds cheering. But President Washington was really happy to go back home. That made me think that being president is really hard, so people have to do it for some reason."

"That is exactly right, Cam," I said softly. "What do you think that reason is?"

Cam looked at Freedom, who smiled at him encouragingly. He said, "I think because he cares about people, like his friends. Oh, and Nelly and Wash and Mrs. Washington. I think maybe it's like my dad. He believes that being a Marine is good for the country, but I know he misses us."

"Yes, that is right. I understood the President's words the

same way. He clearly wanted to go home but he also felt he had a duty to his country," I said.

"But he left in the end, Mr. Revere," Freedom added.

"But that's because he cared about the country more than himself," Cam said. "He gave up the glory and stuff so he could teach people how to have a president."

The sun was rising then, casting long shadows on the path.

Looking at Cam and Freedom, I was surprised how quickly I was overcome with emotion. I felt warmth in my eyes. As the sun warmed the ground around us, I thought of the seeds planted from the early days of our founding. The seeds had grown into the country we know today. George Washington had given us the greatest gift. He sacrificed so freedom and democracy could begin. It could so easily have gone another way.

"Mr. Revere, what's wrong?" Cam asked. He was pulling on my coat sleeve.

"Oh nothing, buddy," I said. "Just some allergies. Must be the hay in the stables." I patted him softly on the back.

Just then, Liberty pushed through the door and whispered, "The area is secure, Captain." He tried to salute and then looked around the stable. "Hey, where's President Washington?"

"He told Mr. Revere he had to go. It was an important day," said Freedom.

Liberty looked at me with his head tilted to one side.

"Yes, President Washington is on his way to President John Adams's inauguration," I said.

We made our way to an open space and headed back to modern day.

The Mount Rushmore National Memorial features sixty-foot sculptures of Presidents Washington, Jefferson, Roosevelt, and Lincoln. Have you ever been to visit this national treasure?

Chapter 7

The next morning, back in modern day, we couldn't have our normal breakfast campaign meeting because I had a dentist appointment. Liberty was so upset by this news, he convinced me to stop by Boston Bagels at lunch to pick him up some garlic and onion bagels to go.

"Revere, you are super-duper, special," Liberty said as we walked to Manchester Middle. "Wow, I am one lucky horse. The luckiest of the lucky, yum, bagels. By the way, what do you call a dentist in the army?"

I looked at Liberty with eyes squinted, waiting for the answer.

"A drill sergeant!" Liberty laughed wildly.

I smiled, and then began thinking of questions for our American Adventurers club meeting. As I entered the classroom, Liberty popped his nose in the window holding a red, white, and blue sign in his teeth that read "NTEF."

"Our good buddy Mr. Liberty is here to help announce

our next game. Who can tell me what we are going to play?" I smiled, looking around the room. Liberty and I had fun making signs the night before.

"NTEF?" asked the young girl sitting next to Freedom. "What's that?"

I replied, "It is the latest game hit. You guys haven't heard of it?" Liberty nodded his head up and down in agreement. The class looked at me with eyebrows raised. "The game is called *Name That Election Fact*," I said.

Cam looked at me smirking. "I haven't heard of it."

"Just wait, Cam. It just so happens NTEF is sweeping the nation. You heard it here first. Today, our American Adventurers meeting, tomorrow, nationwide!"

The class laughed as Liberty held up, in his teeth, questions about the national election. We played several rounds before my digital watch told me it was time to wrap for the day.

"Bravo, first place goes to Freedom." I handed her a coupon for a free music download.

As the students were walking out of the classroom, Tommy came up to me and said, "Mr. Revere, I have an idea."

I looked up and said, "Sure, what about?"

Tommy replied, "My coach puts us through practice drills when he wants us to improve a certain skill. I think we should put Cam through a speech drill. He's got his big speech coming up."

"I have it on my calendar," Freedom added. "It's getting close now, less than two weeks."

"What did you have in mind?" I asked.

Tommy turned around and looked at Cam with a grin. "I think we should drill you with interviews," he said. "Freedom

and I can pretend we're reporters and ask you a bunch of questions. And then you have to answer them like you were being interviewed by a real TV station."

"Sounds cool. Okay, I'm in," said Cam. "But don't you have football practice?"

"Nope, not today. Today, Freedom and I are news reporters," replied Tommy.

"I love the idea! The only problem is, Freedom already left. You'd better hurry up and catch her. I'll meet you in the back by the basketball courts as soon as I find Liberty," I said.

Cam and Tommy raced out the classroom door.

As soon as we all gathered by the basketball courts, Tommy took charge, showing off his quarterback leadership skills. "Okay, Cam, stand in front of that line on the court and face us like you're speaking in front of an audience," said Tommy. "Freedom and I will sit here and pretend we're at the White House in the reporter room and we are official reporters."

"You mean the briefing room, right, Tommy?" asked Liberty. "That's where all the reporters hang out at the White House."

I shook my head, surprised as I often am by Liberty.

"Oh yeah, there. Thanks, Liberty. We want to be legit reporters." Tommy smiled.

He cleared his throat and counted down, "Three, two, one . . ." His voice changed to a deep newscaster voice: "This is Tommy, TOMY Eyewitness News. Mr. President-elect, what do you plan to do in your first month as president of Manchester Middle School?"

Cam paused for a second and replied, "Um, okay, so, yes . . . I want to improve the lunch in the cafeteria. I mean, chicken is good for you and all, but every other day is kinda crazy."

The James S. Brady Press Briefing Room at the White House.
Have you seen this room on TV? Can you imagine Freedom and Tommy
in these seats, firing questions at President Cam?

"What kind of lunches?" Freedom asked, holding on to an imaginary microphone.

Tommy nudged her shoulder and whispered in her ear.

"Oh yes, right." Then, in her best newscaster voice she said, "This is Freedom from FRDM News. What kind of lunch options are you thinking of?"

Cam stood tall and said, "So I was thinking it could be fun stuff that matched the day of the week. Like restaurants have Mashed Potato Mondays or Taco Tuesdays. That kind of stuff." His response had already improved from the first question.

Freedom smiled and said, "Oh, yum. I love tacos. I wish I could go to Manchester Middle for lunch." She looked around with a smile.

Tommy raised his hand. "Food sounds good. What else do you plan to do in your first month?"

Cam paused as if he were searching for a thought, then said, "Well, I really want to improve school spirit. I was thinking we could have a Manchester Middle Spirit Day. Like, everyone at the school could wear the same color and meet on the football field for one big school team huddle."

Tommy nodded and pretended to write detailed notes in an imaginary reporter notebook.

Freedom asked in a deep voice, "As a follow-up, how will you get everyone to go to Spirit Day? What if they don't want to go?"

Cam looked at all of us with a frown, then smiled. "Got it. The Manchester Lion can go from class to class during Spirit Day and get everyone fired up with some dance moves, a song and some tricks. I think everyone will be pumped. Oh, and we could say that on that special day we could have prizes for kids with the best outfits with our school colors."

Tommy and Freedom looked impressed. They spent the next ten minutes firing off questions at Cam. His confidence grew with each question. It was clear Cam had really thought through the ideas and had valid reasons for them.

I observed silently.

When they were done I said, "Super job, Cam."

"You mean, 'Mr. President,' " Cam said, smiling back.

I nodded. I was happy to see him feeling good about his interview.

Suddenly, out of nowhere, Elizabeth and several of her minion cheerleaders came circling around the side of the building. They moved in one line like a marching band. All were wearing bright pink *Vote for Elizabeth* shirts and carrying large campaign buttons with her picture on them.

"If it isn't the Loser Crew from Loserville," Elizabeth said, casting her eyes from side to side.

Cam jerked his head around at the sound of the familiar voice. He looked shocked.

Before I could say anything, Freedom piped up and said, "Why don't you just leave us alone?"

"Too bad, so sad," said Elizabeth. "I am going to be your next president. You'll be seeing me a lot. I even heard that Cam is voting for me."

Her crew guffawed behind her.

"I'm not voting for you," said Cam, folding his arms. "I have a strategy to beat you, Elizabeth."

"Oh, I know all about your strategy," she replied. "And I hope

your speech is better than yesterday. Oh, that's right, you were speech-*less*." More laughter.

"Elizabeth, what are you doing?" I asked.

The girls flicked their hair in unison.

Elizabeth said, "Duh, we're spying. And, Cam, before you embarrass yourself again, just quit."

Cam bit his bottom lip, but did not say anything. Who knew how long she'd been listening.

"Speaking of embarrassing." Elizabeth directed her gaze at Freedom. "It's nice to see that last year's fashion is still in vogue. Really great jeans. Did you get those at the grocery store, Freedom?"

"That is enough . . ." I started.

Freedom stared at Elizabeth. "Why don't you go get some ideas of your own, and stop trying to steal Cam's. If you took some time to actually work on helping students instead of being mean to them, you wouldn't have to spy."

Elizabeth glared at Freedom.

Without warning, Liberty appeared out of thin air, right behind Elizabeth and her cheer goons.

"Eww, what's that smell?" asked Elizabeth.

"Behind you," said Freedom, with a big smile.

Liberty exhaled deeply. Apparently, he had saved his garlic and onion bagels as an afternoon snack, because even I could smell his breath from ten feet away.

The girls clung to each other, gagging, as they scrambled away toward the parking lot.

"Grrr," Cam groaned, kicking his foot across the court. "She better not have heard my lunch ideas." His confidence seemed to have faded away.

"Thanks for coming when you did, Liberty," said Freedom. "I'd rub your nose, but I think I'm safer over here."

"Revere, I think I need more of those breath mints," Liberty admitted.

"You think?" I replied.

The next day, Team Cam piled out of Freedom's grandfather's car in front of Boston Bagels. Cam texted me to tell me he was totally over Elizabeth's spying and he wasn't going to think about it anymore. I wondered how long that would last.

Freedom waved to her grandfather and raced over to our table quicker than both boys. "Girl power!" she gleefully shouted.

Liberty grinned. "Way to go, Freedom. I stupendously, monumentally, abundantly admire your running ability. Was that a personal best?" He looked at her as if he were asking a profound question.

"Um, it was pretty quick, I guess." She blushed, and plopped down in her chair at the usual outside table. Cam and Tommy sat, too.

Liberty continued, "By the way, Revere, I don't know if you noticed that I haven't mentioned carrots, apples, peppermints, or bagels in the last two hours." He was leaning over the edge of the table, ignoring passersby who were whispering and pointing at him from a distance. "Not that I'm counting or anything. So, how many bagels are you ordering for me? How about a dozen, you know, one for every month?"

I laughed as Liberty gave me puppy dog eyes. "Liberty, you are planning to take the twelve-month stock and eat them right now, aren't you?"

Liberty looked at me, squinting. "What do you mean by *now?*

If you are an American over eighteen years old, you have the right to vote! Amendments 15, 19, and 26 protect this right for all.

Like now, now, or now and later?" He was clearly trying to confuse me.

I just shook my head and laughed.

"You got lucky on that race, Freedom," Tommy said. "If I had my cleats on I would have won easily."

"Yeah, Freedom," Cam added. "I was wearing my campaign shoes. Makes it tough to get traction."

Freedom shook her head and said, "Whatever, guys. I'm on a winning streak. First the history game and now this."

"The only race I'm running from now on is my presidential race," Cam joked.

Everyone dove into their bagel sandwiches. "I don't know about you, but all of this time travel makes me hungry," Cam said between bites.

Liberty nodded and muttered with cheeks full of bagels, "Yum."

I said, "I'm sorry you missed our trip to 1797, Tommy."

"Yeah, it was totally cool," Cam said. "I mean, I didn't get to see President Washington talk in front of a large crowd like Mr. Revere promised, but it was fun anyway." Cam laughed. "Just joking, Mr. Revere."

Tommy asked, "So, no speech?"

"No, it was a Farewell Address that was printed in the newspapers. He was saying goodbye, basically," Cam said. "Kind of a bummer."

"People in 1797 were also unhappy about it," I added. "After the ceremony George Washington made his way through massive crowds who wanted to catch one final glimpse of the first president. They had tears in their eyes and begged him not to go but he said nothing as he walked. This made the crowd even more emotional. Finally he turned, and they saw tears in his eyes, as he left with his family to Mount Vernon."

Everyone was quiet.

"But I have some good news. Since you couldn't come with us, Tommy, I wanted to bring a little bit of our trip to you." I pulled out two white mini-speakers and put them on the table.

I started to unlock my smartphone, when Tommy pointed and said, "Those are cool! I didn't know they had mini-speaker souvenirs from the 1700s. Awesome." He smiled.

"Good one." Freedom gave a thumbs-up.

I took a sip of my hot coffee and said, "Okay, here we go. Come closer, guys. This is a quick audio sample of George Washington's Farewell Address, read by a modern-day actor. I think it brings it to life."

The crew nodded.

I hit play. Instantaneously, the famous words streamed out of the little speakers. Everyone leaned in. For an instant, it felt like I was back in the stables hearing President Washington himself.

> *Interwoven as is the love of liberty with every liga-*
> *ment of your hearts, no recommendation of mine is*
> *necessary to fortify or confirm the attachment. . . .*

I paused the recording. "Here, President Washington is saying that he did not need to speak about freedom in his Farewell Address, because it was already in the hearts of every American."

Right then, a familiar voice said, "That is one of my favorite speeches of all time."

We turned to see Joseph standing up against the window, holding a to-go cup of coffee. He was dressed in his usual button-down checked shirt and khaki pants.

I said, "Good morning, Congressman."

He smiled with bright white teeth and said, "Good morning. I see you have expanded your group."

"Yes, indeed. Please let me introduce you to the members of Cam's campaign team." I introduced Freedom and then Tommy.

"Don't forget my campaign advisor, Liberty," said Cam. He turned to where Liberty was standing and patted Liberty's nose.

I smiled and said, "This is Joseph, a former congressman from our state and a regular here at our campaign headquarters. Congressman, we are listening to George Washington's Farewell Address so we can talk about the meaning of the words. Also, Cam is learning how to craft his big speech that he will present in front of the school assembly."

Joseph nodded, stepping closer. "This is absolutely brilliant." He paused and thought for a moment. "Hearing those famous words takes me back to my years in Congress. Do you know that this very speech, the 1797 Farewell Address, has been read every year in the Senate? No other Senate tradition is stronger. This speech is up there with the Declaration of Independence and the Constitution."

"Oh cool," said Cam. "I didn't know it was so important before. Actually, I never even heard of it."

"I'm sorry to hear that," Joseph said, "but isn't it nice to know about it now?"

Cam nodded.

Freedom and Tommy looked politely at the Congressman.

Joseph asked, "Did you guys hear the part where President

Washington was speaking about *factions?* Among other things he was warning about the dangers of political parties, which are groups of people who try to get someone elected to get certain things done."

"Oh, yeah, we had a game about those," Cam said. "Democrat and Republican, right? Blue and red states?"

"Absolutely, well done. You must have a pretty sharp teacher," Joseph said, winking in my direction. "Do you know what animal is the symbol of each party?"

Cam's team looked at each other and shrugged their shoulders.

"The donkey is the symbol of the Democrat Party and the elephant is the symbol of the Republican Party."

"That's kind of like a mascot, right?" Freedom said. "Cam is our school mascot. He's our mighty lion." She gave him a fist bump.

"Wow, you are a busy young man. You are all clearly a very talented bunch," said Joseph, smiling. He crossed his arms in a relaxed way. "In the Farewell Address you heard that Washington did not want political parties or *factions*, right?"

Freedom nodded.

"Despite Washington's warnings, two parties formed even before he left the presidency. Back then, they were called the *Federalists* and *Anti-Federalists*, and both had their own views about how the country should be run. Vice President John Adams formed one party and Secretary of State Thomas Jefferson formed the other. Over hundreds of years these parties shifted. Now we have the Democrats and Republicans."

Liberty was chomping on another bagel. I sensed he wanted to jump in and talk about something, but he held his tongue.

"Anyway, enough about political parties," the Congressman said, turning to Cam. "How is everything going with your campaign?"

There was quiet around the table, except for the sound of Liberty's teeth clicking together.

Everyone stayed silent, so I said, "Cam was having a little trouble delivering his speech. He froze a bit at first. So, we decided to do a question-and-answer session as a drill, to sharpen Cam's plans about what he would do as president. Later, we found out that Elizabeth was eavesdropping the whole time. Cam is worried she will steal his good ideas."

Cam shook his head and rolled his eyes at the mention of Elizabeth.

This is such an emotional roller coaster, I thought.

Congressman Joseph said, "You know, that kind of thing happens all of the time, unfortunately, even at the national election level. To beat Elizabeth, you need to make sure your ideas are well thought through and can be clearly explained to other students. Then put the thoughts into your speech, and communicate them to the students better than she does. The more people who know and agree with what you stand for, and what you plan to do as president, the more votes you will receive."

Cam looked up at the Congressman, like he was absorbing every word.

Joseph continued. "You are probably thinking this is easier said than done. But remember, I am an old goat. I have been there. The best advice I can give is to practice, practice, and practice. Stand in front of the mirror and watch to make sure you don't play with your hair or fidget with your pockets. Also, no one pays attention for long, so you need to get right to the point with lots of oomph. You must catch them in a short period of time."

Tommy repeated, "Oomph," and laughed.

"And one more thing, don't just go after one group, like Elizabeth's so-called *cool kids*. Who defines cool, anyway? Your message should speak to everyone. You should reach out to as many students as you can, cool or not cool," said the Congressman.

"That is fantastic advice. Thank you very much," I said.

Congressman Joseph took a big sip of his coffee. "Cam, did you happen to see the presidential debates on TV last night? At the beginning and the end the candidates gave speeches."

Cam shrugged his shoulders and said, "No, Mom told me the debates were on like every channel but I was thinking about my own campaign."

Freedom said, "My grandpa had the debates on at our house. I didn't really watch them because I was doing my homework but I kept hearing this cool music and the announcer would say, 'Back to the prime-time debates,' in a really deep voice." She hummed the music from the newscast.

"Yes, all of the debates do have announcers, catchy tunes, and TV graphics. That is great humming," said the Congressman, smiling at Freedom.

"It may be worth your time to watch a repeat of those speeches, and determine which you liked best, and why," the Congressman went on encouragingly. "Note which ones you liked, and made you want to vote."

Cam nodded seriously, and wrote a note in his playbook.

"Hope that helps a little bit. I know you are going to be great. Now, I should be on my way. I'm retired but seem busier than I was before."

He waved as he left the table, and we waved back, including Liberty, who nodded.

A few feet from the table Joseph called back, "And by the way, free refills are great. You can't go wrong with that." He pointed to his cup. "Cam, you may want to throw free refills into your election strategy." Joseph made his way slowly to his car.

"That is great advice! How about you add those to your playbook: play six—*Develop and practice your speech regularly* and play seven—*Focus on a strategy to get votes*," I said. "Also, I thought of some others we learned from President Washington's farewell. How about: play eight—*Use your leadership skills to adjust your plan to what is thrown at you*, and play nine—*Know that the presidency is bigger than one person, and service to others is more important than glory*."

"Okay," Cam said as he wrote.

Liberty let out a big sigh. "Phew, I was dying to jump in there but knew Joseph would be pretty surprised that I could talk. So let's get serious. Down to business. Focused," he said.

Amazingly, we all kept a straight face.

"The Congressman is a sly fox. He has some very good points," Liberty said. "Free refills sounds good to me. As campaign advisor, I agree we need to focus on getting votes. I mean, that is the name of the game. When is the vote, by the way?"

I replied, "According to the original election rules, it is coming up in ten days. The big speeches are the day before. This will be Cam's only chance to speak to the entire student body before the vote. Like Congressman Joseph said, it needs to be great."

"Okay, okay, we are short on time," Liberty said. "Let me think, who can we reach that Elizabeth is ignoring? Horses, birds, caterpillars . . . oh no, wait, they can't vote. Let me get back to you once I mull it over."

Freedom piped up: "The Congressman told us we shouldn't just go after the cool kids like Elizabeth is doing. We should reach out to everyone."

Tommy said, "I can ask more of the football guys. There's a ton of them and they think Elizabeth is annoying. I'll get the buzz going around the team."

"Cool," said Cam. "Thanks, guys."

"What about Ed?" I asked, not having heard an update in a while.

"I almost forgot about Ed," said Cam, "but I will talk to him today. When I saw him last he said he was almost done with my election song. He's teaching the whole band."

"Okay, good. The football team, the band, who else can you think of to help you?" I asked.

"I can talk to everyone in the art classes," said Freedom. "I can show them the campaign posters I did."

"Brilliant Team Cam, B-b-b Brilliant!" Liberty exclaimed.

I looked around to make sure no one else at the bagel shop could hear.

"This sounds like a play for the playbook to me, right?" said Tommy.

"You know what, spot-on, Tommy. Let's add that to the list. We can make this one play ten: *Expand your voting groups to increase votes.*"

Cam wrote a note. "Got it!" He flipped through his playbook and said, "This is what we have so far: *know rules, sign up, be a good leader, pick good team, communicate, change plan if need to,* create and practice speech, make presidency bigger than myself, get votes by expanding to new groups."

Just then, a lightbulb went off in my head. "I think I know the perfect couple who can help us," I said.

"Really? Who?" asked Cam, eagerly.

I spoke softly, to make sure no one leaving the bagel shop heard. "So you know how we keep talking about strategies and plays? John and his wife, Abigail Adams, were some of the best political strategists in our history. After George Washington, John Adams was the second president. He used his planning skills to win the really difficult presidential election of 1796. They focused on reaching as many people as possible with their message and vision for the country."

Cam looked intrigued.

"I like that name, Abigail. It sounds very nice but formal, too," Freedom said, sweetly.

I turned to face her and said, "You know what, Freedom? Abigail was very much as her name sounds. She was extremely dignified, strong, and brilliant. Abigail was a great partner to John Adams, and vice versa. Together, they worked on his presidential election strategy and also on being great leaders."

"Wow, that is really cool," Freedom said.

"Indeed, she was truly remarkable," I added. "Besides being the president's wife, she was also a mother and caregiver for the ill. Mrs. Adams managed the finances on their farm, bought government bonds, and sold materials for a profit."

"So amazing!" said Freedom. "I'm already impressed, and I haven't even met her."

Liberty nodded in agreement.

"Yes, Mrs. Adams was quite incredible. You could say she was ahead of her time," I said.

"What does it mean that she was ahead of her time?" Cam asked.

"Good question," I replied. "It means that her ideas and the way she behaved were *revolutionary* in her time. While her husband, John Adams, was fighting a revolution with the British, she was fighting her own battle for the rights of women, African-Americans, the poor, and others."

Cam looked at me with wide eyes, listening intently.

"In 1797, sadly, women could not yet vote, and slavery still existed in the United States. As you can see, people at the time, just like now, were far from perfect."

Freedom and Cam looked on quietly.

I took a deep breath and continued, "But following from people like Mrs. Adams, eventually Americans amended the U.S. Constitution to make sure that all people could vote, and slavery was abolished. Improvements are continually being made, and I believe the best days are ahead of us as a country."

Cam clapped his hands together once and said, "I really want to meet them. They sound supersmart."

Liberty agreed. "Let's go talk to President and Mrs. Adams about their strategy and how they got votes. Well, I mean I won't do the talking, but you know."

"Yeah, we need all the strategy help we can get. Elizabeth just can't win! Am I right, team?" said Cam energetically.

"Agree! We have to win because Elizabeth doesn't care about anyone but herself, and would be a horrible president," added Freedom.

Cam pumped his fist like he was getting ready for a big game. "Let's go, Team Cam!"

Liberty said, "All right, right, right. I am liking the fire, Cam. Look out, ladies and gentlemen, call the fire department. My main man, President Cam, is on fire!"

We all laughed.

Chapter 8

fter school, the Manchester Lions football team left for a game with rivals across town. Of course, Tommy, as the quarterback, had to go. Cam also went, as the team mascot. Seeing him getting on the bus wearing his Lion costume was hilarious.

"I wish Cam and Tommy could come with us," Freedom said.

"Me, too," I said.

"Me, three," said Liberty. "Hey, we'll be the Three Musketeers jumping back in time."

Freedom looked uncomfortable in her colonial clothes as we stood under the shade of our favorite oak tree near Manchester Middle School. "If Elizabeth sees me she'll laugh at my hat, but whatever, she laughs at me every day."

"You look *très chic,* if you ask me," said Liberty. "That's French for stylish."

"Thanks, Liberty, I feel better." Freedom made a silly face as if she were modeling.

I said, "Oh, before I forget, Cam asked me to bring his playbook so Freedom could take some notes. I'll put it in Liberty's saddlebag for safekeeping."

As I opened the bag, a carrot poked out. I gave it to Liberty and said, "Liberty, start your engine. We are going to see Abigail Adams, whom we first met in 1790. This time in Massachusetts on March 4, 1797."

Liberty scratched his hoof on the ground like he was kick-starting his internal time-travel motorcycle. "*Rush, rush, rushing to history!*" he yelled, and the purple and yellow swirling colors appeared as we jumped through the time portal.

We jumped through the portal and softly landed on the dirt behind a large, two-story colonial home with shuttered windows and a large chimney. Chickens flapped away from us, no doubt spooked by the time portal.

"Well done, Liberty," I said, sliding off the saddle, and then helped Freedom jump down. It felt like we were in the countryside.

"Yeah, nice jumping, Liberty," said Freedom.

I looked around and said, "Today is a special day, because it's the day the second president of the United States, John Adams, was inaugurated." I started to pace back and forth. "We're about to meet Abigail Adams, his wife. History tells us she couldn't attend her husband's inauguration because she was tending to a long list of responsibilities on the farm, which included caring for her mother, who was quite ill."

"Mr. Revere, you seem a little nervous," said Freedom.

"Well, it's probably because I am a little nervous. I haven't really come up with an excuse for being here."

Freedom smiled, looking around. "I can't wait to ask her about her animals. Hey, look, Liberty already met some friends."

Across the yard, Liberty was standing next to a fence with two sheepdogs on the other side. The large hairy dogs looked like happy lions jumping up on the fence with delight, with long bangs completely covering their faces. A few sheep grazed near the fence and were quickly herded away by the sheepdogs. Liberty walked one way and the sheepdogs instantly followed. He quickly turned around and walked the other way and they bounded near his hooves on the other side of the fence. It was funny to watch.

"Those dogs are adorable. But how can they see with all that hair in their eyes?" Freedom asked.

"Great question. We will have to ask Liberty to find out. Maybe he speaks sheepdog," I said, smiling. "They should keep him entertained for a while."

I looked around and saw green pathways, trees, and stone walls, leading between the main building and a smaller building with a slanted roof. A carriage sat in front and large trees cast a pleasant shade all around. Small, rolling green hills framed the property.

"Can we go meet Abigail Adams now?" Freedom asked. "Maybe she'll sign her name in Cam's playbook."

I nodded, and we boldly pressed forward, following a wooden fence to the front of the house.

There were lots of people moving around the farm grounds. They seemed to come from all different walks of life. Some were older, some younger; some appeared to belong on a farm while another looked like they would be more comfortable at a bank.

All around, there were tools, animals in pens, clothes drying on lines, and little tables filled with odds and ends.

As we neared the main house, I pointed. "There she is. The First Lady of the United States of America, Abigail Adams."

Mrs. Adams looked focused as she moved back and forth across the yard, throwing her large skirt to one side, kicking up dust as she walked. She seemed to be engaged in multiple conversations.

"Her brown dress is so pretty," said Freedom. "How can she look so nice, running around this farm?"

I replied, "Abigail Adams is an incredible woman. From everything I've read, she is known as being brilliant, accomplished, and talented. And as you can see, she can multitask really well."

Freedom's eyes were wide. "Wow, I can't wait to meet her," she said.

We walked up to Mrs. Adams. Immediately, her dark brown eyes stared directly into mine. She had a dominating presence despite her outwardly soft and elegant appearance. "Mr. Revere, we meet again," she said seriously. "Now, the last time you appeared out of the blue, it was at the President's House, with your student. What brings you to visit this time?" Incredibly, Mrs. Adams remembered our last meeting in detail, despite seven years having passed.

I froze for a second, unsure how to reply.

"Mrs. Adams," I said with a formal bow, "it is a pleasure to see you again. We came here to congratulate you on your husband's election win."

"Who is *we*?" Mrs. Adams asked sharply, her eyes not releasing mine.

I anxiously replied, "Oh, this is my student, Freedom."

Freedom looked up at both of us.

"She has read so much about you and admires you greatly."

Mrs. Adams took her eyes off me and focused on Freedom. As she did, she softened and leaned in. "Why, thank you very much, young lady. I certainly appreciate your admiration. But I am especially thrilled to hear that you are reading. It is extremely important."

Freedom smiled shyly as Mrs. Adams continued: "I love your name; it is really beautiful, and meaningful. How did your parents name you *Freedom?*"

Freedom shrugged politely. "Thank you. I think it is because I was born on July Fourth."

Mrs. Adams smiled happily. "Wonderful, simply wonderful!"

The knot in my stomach began to release.

Just then, a tall man approached us wearing a full brown suit and tie. *A bit dressed-up for the farm,* I thought.

"Mrs. Adams, I've left the bond information you asked for in the study. Please let me know if you'd like to move forward with the deal," the man said, then took off his hat to gesture goodbye and left.

A second later, a young lady carrying large jugs passed by and said, "Mrs. Adams, I have the fresh milk you requested and will place it in the storage area."

The First Lady nodded.

Everyone seemed to have a comment or request for Mrs. Adams as they rotated past. She handled each with a dignified response and didn't seem the least bit flustered.

Mrs. Adams turned back at Freedom and said, "I certainly do not want to be rude, young lady, but I am in the middle of a few things. I am preparing to leave in the morning by carriage to meet my husband, John, in Philadelphia. But you're welcome to follow me as I complete my tasks. We can talk more if you do not mind the distractions."

Freedom nodded excitedly.

Mrs. Adams held Freedom's hand and together they walked. Chairs rested on the front porch of the house, giving an overall peaceful sense to the busy scene. Freedom looked back at me, smiling brightly as I followed behind.

Mrs. Adams and Freedom talked as they moved from one project to the next. I tried my best to keep up as they weaved between chickens and moving carts. Even though the First Lady was so busy, she made time for everyone.

After checking on the cows, we walked up to a wooden gate where a young boy was standing. Mrs. Adams passed him a sealed envelope and said, "Please deliver this to my husband, thank you." He raced away with the letter and some coins Mrs. Adams had given him.

She turned to us and said, "My husband is in Philadelphia and he works tirelessly in service to the country. I try to write as often as possible to share a thought or two. Sometimes he takes my advice. The young lad is taking my latest letter to Philadelphia."

"I love getting letters," Freedom said. "It's a lot better than e—"

I knew she was about to say *emails* so I interrupted and said, "Yes, a lot better than eating. Yes, a lot better to receive a letter than to eat. I really like to wait to receive a letter and then read it while I eat."

"Yes, I suppose letters are good when you are eating, thank you, Mr. Revere." Mrs. Adams looked at me skeptically. "I love writing letters to John. We must have written thousands back

and forth." She looked closely at Freedom. "Remember, an education, particularly for girls, is incredibly important. We have so much to add to the conversation. I always remind the President to *remember the ladies* in law and government."

Freedom seemed to hang on every word.

"Mr. Revere, you have a fine student here. I can see her becoming president of the United States one day."

I knew that at this time in history, women did not have the opportunities of today, making Mrs. Adams even more impressive.

"I agree completely," I said.

"Now, I must go inside and make further preparations, but it has been a true pleasure spending the morning with you. I will be sure to tell the President you visited."

"Thank you, Mrs. Adams; the pleasure was ours." We waved goodbye and began following the fence back to Liberty.

"I really like Mrs. Adams," Freedom said. "Can we go see President Adams, too?"

"That's a great idea," I replied. "Let's see what Liberty is up to before we get going."

We found Liberty where we left him, playing with the sheepdogs. They stood on either side of the fence, tossing tufts of grass back and forth with their noses. The dogs barked in harmony like they were singing a special song.

"Excuse me, Liberty, I need to speak with you," I said.

Liberty turned and whined, "Is it time to go already? I'm just warming up for my next big spike. Who knew grass volleyball could be so fun? Wait, wait for it, Revere, check this out."

Liberty took a big chomp of grass and dropped it over the fence with his mouth. The grass landed right on a sheepdog's head.

[JA to AA]

Philadelphia March 5 1797

XXX 211
II 3244

My dearest Friend, your dearest Friend never had a more trying day than yesterday. A Solemn Scene it was indeed and it was made more affecting to me, by the Presence of the General, whose Countenance was as serene and unclouded as the day. He seem'd to enjoy a Tryumph over me. Methought I heard him think Ay! I am fairly out and you fairly in! See which of Us will be happiest. When the Ceremony was over he came and made me a visit and cordially congratulated me and wished my Administration might be happy Successful and honourable.

It is now settled that I am to go into his House. It is whispered that he intends to take french Leave tomorrow. I shall write you, as fast as we proceed.

My Chariot is finished and I made my first appearance in it yesterday. It is simple but elegant enough. My horses are young but clever.

In the Chamber of the House of Representatives was a Multitude as great as the Space could contain, and I believe Scarcely a dry Eye but Washingtons. The Sight of the Sun Setting full orbed and another rising tho less Splendid, was a novelty.

C. J. Ellsworth administered the oath and with great Energy. Judges Cushing, Willson and Iredell were present. Many Ladies.

I had not Slept well the night before and did not sleep well the night after. I was unwell and I did not know whether I Should get through or not. I did however. How the Business was received I know not only I have been told that Masas the Treaty publisher Said he Should loose nothing by the Change for he never heard Such a Sound in Publick in his Life. All agree that taken all together it was the Sublimest Thing ever exhibited in America. I am my dearest friend most affectionately & kindly yours

John Adams

President John Adams wrote this letter to Abigail on the day of his inauguration. It is one of thousands they wrote to each other while apart.

Freedom laughed. "That's so funny."

"Score one for Big Horsey!" Liberty announced. "Woop-woop. Oh yeah." The sheepdogs seemed to look at each other quizzically.

I leaned into Liberty's ear and whispered.

"Got it, Captain," Liberty said. "I'm on it, right after I win this final point."

I laughed to myself, thinking only Liberty could pick up a game of grass volleyball entirely out of the blue.

After the game, Liberty bid goodbye to his friends, who darted back toward a group of meandering sheep.

We hoisted ourselves onto Liberty's back. When no one was watching, except for a few chickens, Liberty said, *"Rush, rush, rushing to history."* As he galloped toward the portal opening, I yelled, "Do you remember the destination I whispered!"

"Yep, I think so," said Liberty.

The words *I think so* were not what I wanted to hear.

The landing was a little harder than usual. "Sorry about that. But you didn't give me an exact location, so I had to wing it," Liberty said. "But we're here safe and sound in Philadelphia."

I looked to the left and then to the right. A long, dusty dirt road was bordered by tan and green fields. The only thing nearby was what looked to be a tavern, about a hundred yards away next to a small lake.

"Liberty, are you sure we're in Philadelphia?" asked Freedom. Her white cap waved in a cool wind. "When I was in Philadelphia in 1775 it looked a lot different."

Liberty looked around. "That's because in 1775 we

time-jumped to the center of the city. This time, Revere had me jump to a dirt road just outside of the city heading northeast to Massachusetts."

I replied, "Yes, that's because—"

"Wait, what's that sound?" asked Freedom, curiously.

"Don't worry, Freedom," said Liberty, dramatically. "I'll save you."

The noise was coming from somewhere beyond the bend in the road with a small hill on one side.

"Wait," said Freedom, listening carefully. "That sounds like horse hooves, and I think they're coming this way."

Just then, a fast-moving carriage being pulled by two horses came careening around the bend.

"Look out!" I said, pulling Freedom out of the way with both hands. Liberty jumped backward and gave the passing horses a stern glance. My heart was racing. The carriage and horses came to a sharp stop right in front of us, casting a plume of dust into the air.

A chubby, balding man ambled out of the carriage, nearly tripping when his feet hit the dirt road. He was wearing formal brown clothes that appeared a little dusty from the road. "Pardon me, I am so sorry my driver didn't see you. I hope you were not harmed."

My adrenaline was pumping, and I was so concerned for Freedom I barely heard what the man said next.

"I apologize, I am in such a rush. I am trying to surprise my wife before she gets to Philadelphia." He looked nervous and was sweating heavily.

I was grateful for the sincere apology, but before I could

respond I saw another black coach heading southwest coming directly toward us. The previously deserted road now looked like rush-hour traffic.

"Be careful!" I shouted to the oncoming carriage, raising my hands in the air. I pushed Freedom behind me and to the side, and Liberty jumped out of the way.

Dust flew into the air as the carriage swerved. The driver of the new carriage lurched to the side wildly, pulling hard on the reins of the horses. The wheels of the carriage kept spinning as the horses pulled up and finally came to a stop ten feet from us.

The driver released the reins and bowed deeply, removing his hat. He said, "My sincere apologies, sir. We were in a great hurry. The First Lady is hoping to catch the President before he leaves Philadelphia."

Just then a woman's head popped out from the carriage window. She wore a white cap that matched Freedom's and had a serious expression that opened into a wide smile. She pushed open the door and came running down the dirt road toward the heavyset man from the first carriage.

"Mrs. Adams!" said the heavyset man, joyfully.

They rushed into each other's arms and hugged, then kissed, and then whispered to each other.

"Aww, isn't that cute?" Liberty said, softly humming to himself. "So romantic."

Freedom giggled and put her hand over her mouth.

Liberty leaned over and whispered in my ear. "See, I told you I could find the President and First Lady together."

I laughed. President and Mrs. Adams looked over in our direction and headed toward us hand in hand.

This is George Washington's carriage at the Mount Vernon
Museum. John and Abigail Adams rode in similar
carriages while he was president.

Mrs. Adams looked me right in the eye. Surprised, she said, "Mr. Revere, it's rather peculiar that we meet again in the middle of this road. What are you doing out here with my husband?"

She looked kindly at Freedom, who shrugged and looked at me.

I nervously replied, "Good day, Mrs. Adams. It is such a pleasure to see you again."

Hesitantly, Mrs. Adams said, "And you as well, Mr. Revere." She turned to her husband and said, "Mr. Revere came to the farmhouse not too long ago to congratulate us on your presidential victory. This wise young lady is his student, Freedom."

"Fabulous name!" President Adams said, stretching out his hand to shake ours. He smiled widely.

Mrs. Adams winked. "We are on the same page as always, darling. I love her name as well."

Sometimes when I am nervous, I start to talk a lot. This was one of those times. I stuttered, "It is really funny, actually, we, um, we were . . ." I paused as I searched for an idea. And then I saw it. I pointed to the nearby tavern. "The tavern! Yes, we were on our way to this tavern for a midday meal when we almost collided with your husband's carriage." I smiled, feeling pretty good about my answer.

"Oh my, I'm glad no one was hurt," said Mrs. Adams.

After a quiet moment, John Adams, the second president of the United States of America, said, "I don't know about you, but travel makes me quite famished. Perhaps we could rest our horses and have a bite to eat. Of course, we can't stay long. I have some urgent matters to—"

Mrs. Adams kissed her husband on the cheek and smiled. "Certainly these matters can wait for you to spend some time with your wife and my new friends."

He looked longingly at Abigail and said, "Yes, I suppose the members of Congress can wait a little while." He smiled and kissed his wife on the forehead.

Freedom gave me a secret thumbs-up.

"Come, now, let's all have a good meal," said Mrs. Adams.

I bowed to the President and said, "Thank you, sir, we would be delighted to join you." As we walked the short distance to the tavern I had to pinch myself. We were about to have a meal with President John Adams and First Lady Abigail Adams.

"Mr. Revere says he's a history teacher," Mrs. Adams said.

"Yes, and I just want to thank you, Mr. President, for your great service to our country. We know as president you will lead our nation forward in the footsteps of George Washington."

President Adams replied, "Thank you, Mr. Revere, I will certainly try my best. It is not easy to follow the great George Washington. But I plan to serve my country and improve the lives of our people."

As we approached the entrance to the tavern I whispered to Liberty to be on his best behavior. If he stayed outside and did not wander off he would receive some carrot cake. He argued for four slices, but I bargained down to three.

The tavern owner sat us at a large window overlooking the lake.

The president pulled out his pocket watch and then called for the waiter. He said, "Could I please have a copy of the newspapers from today? As many as you have available, *posthaste*, my good man."

"John, please," Mrs. Adams said. "We have guests. Would you mind leaving the affairs of state for a few minutes? You need sustenance in your new capacity as president. Man cannot live on politics alone."

Abigail Adams was the second first lady of the United States.
She was a leader, mother, war reporter, businessperson,
caregiver for the ill, and partner to the president.

John Adams served as the second president of the United States from March 4, 1797, until March 4, 1801. Can you name a few of his leadership qualities?

Freedom sat in her chair politely.

"Of course, Mrs. Adams, or should I say *Mrs. President.*" He smiled and nudged her in the arm. "If you yourself ever gave up politics for a moment, I would be quite shocked."

"On this rare occasion, perhaps you are right, John," she joked. "But for the sake of our guests, let us put our political discussions aside and engage in more pleasant conversation."

President Adams nodded in agreement. Then he began to laugh so loud his voice echoed off the walls of the tavern. It was so contagious I began to laugh myself without knowing the joke. Then Freedom started laughing. Others turned to look as the President said, "Mr. Revere, since we are discussing happier things, let me tell you one brief story about my lovely wife, Abigail, as a young woman."

Mrs. Adams shook her head with a slight smile.

"Years ago, when I was still a young man, I visited Abigail, hoping to court her. Oh, she was as beautiful as she is now. She came from a good family and at first, things were going well. I began to tell some stories and all of a sudden she and her sisters were nothing but *saucy* to me. If you can believe it, she even accused me of being arrogant. Me!" Again, the President laughed and held his stomach.

Mrs. Adams smiled at him with a twinkle in her eye. "You *were* arrogant. You acted as though we were country rubes without an idea of our own. You thought you could teach us everything about the world. Oh, you were truly awful at first."

The President leaned into Mrs. Adams gently.

She added, "But since then, I have worked on you, and you are now far less grumpy and arrogant. In fact, you are close to charming." She smiled with a mischievous grin.

The food arrived and was placed in front of us. Potatoes in a heavy sauce smelled and looked delicious.

The President smiled, then nodded sincerely and said, "Eventually it was Abigail's sauciness and intelligence that I came to love and still do. We have been married for over thirty years now, and every day has been better than the last."

Mrs. Adams looked at her husband sweetly, then shifted to say, "I will have to write that down, Mr. President, as that is one to remember."

"That is so sweet," Freedom said with a soft smile.

As we spoke, it was amazing to watch such a powerful union in action. John and Abigail were clearly partners, strong individually and even stronger united.

As we finished our meals, I wondered how they managed to remain focused on their goals for the country. I asked, "I know that you faced great obstacles during your campaign. Which was the hardest to overcome?"

"Yes, Mr. Revere, there were many difficulties," Mrs. Adams said with a weary look. "Too many to count, in fact. I suppose the biggest challenge was our separation from Thomas Jefferson, who was our close friend. We lived together in France, and I took care of his children. But during George Washington's presidency Thomas Jefferson formed a new party, causing conflict. No one wants to return to a monarchy, but we have different views about the future of the country."

President Adams nodded. "That is correct. Two parties, the right party and the wrong party," he said seriously.

A man dressed in a white shirt with a fluffy collar came to our table to clear our plates. A few moments later, a different man brought over a hot pot of tea and warm biscuits.

Mrs. Adams half-smiled and returned to a serious tone. "As in any competition, the two parties did not agree on many topics at all. During the election of 1796, it was very bitter, with both sides using the newspapers to attack each other. It was truly ugly. Luckily, John won."

Freedom leaned over and whispered, "It sounds just like Elizabeth and Cam." She poured some tea in a ceramic cup.

Casually, I added, "I believe President Adams worked with Thomas Jefferson on the Declaration of Independence."

Mrs. Adams continued, "Yes, absolutely correct. John, do you remember the letter I sent to you when you were helping to write the Declaration of Independence reminding you to *remember the ladies?*"

"How could I forget?" the President said. "You wrote that when we were creating the laws of the country. You said we should remember to be more generous to women than our ancestors were. You were afraid of unlimited power in the hands of men, as I recall. You even said there may be a rebellion if women do not have a voice. Very strong words, indeed."

She smiled. "Yes, I recognize I have strong views but still believe that all men would be tyrants if they could."

"Not me, my dear, not me," John Adams said, sipping his tea.

Mrs. Adams laughed. "Of course not you, John." They snuggled up together for a second.

"My wife is a genius, truly. She always has a well-thought-out argument, and we go back and forth on many topics. After we speak, we often come to agreement. She has a gift of making the complex simple. Whereas, I suppose I have the talent of making the complex more complex."

Mrs. Adams smiled widely and they both laughed.

Freedom and I joined in.

"May I ask, with all of these challenges, how do you know best what to do?"

Mrs. Adams motioned for the President to try a biscuit, then said, "To answer your question, Mr. Revere, the absolute truth is, and I think John would agree, that we do not know. We simply have an inner faith that guides us and reminds us to fight for our principles, no matter the opposition."

Freedom looked at Mrs. Adams as if she were a princess in a castle. Her eyes observed every movement.

President Adams added, "Mrs. Adams is correct. Our overriding hope and goal has been to serve our country. We have never lost sight of that despite everything that has occurred."

Mrs. Adams lightly clapped her hands together once and said, "Freedom, I do apologize. We must be boring you with all this political discussion."

"I like it!" Freedom exclaimed.

Just then a flash of brown distracted me. I turned to look out the window and gasped. Liberty had run full speed and jumped into the lake, cannonball-style. The water splashed in the air like a tall water fountain. Liberty bounced up and down, making big waves around him. He dunked his head, then popped out and shook water from his eyes. I tried not to look but couldn't help it. I thought, *Liberty, you are truly one of a kind.*

Freedom looked at me with wide eyes.

President and Mrs. Adams were sipping tea and eating biscuits, so I looked over their shoulders. Liberty had made it back to shore and was shaking himself dry.

Freedom had to cover her mouth to stifle a laugh.

Mrs. Adams put down her teacup, raised her eyebrows, and

First Two-Party Election

1796

THOMAS JEFFERSON
DEMOCRATIC REPUBLIC

In 1796, John Adams won the first two-party
election, but Thomas Jefferson won in 1800.
Are elections similar today?

1
7
9
6

JOHN ADAMS
FEDERALIST

ELECTION OF 1796

TERRITORIES

In the 1796 election, John Adams defeated Thomas Jefferson
by only three votes, and Jefferson became vice
president. That is different from today!

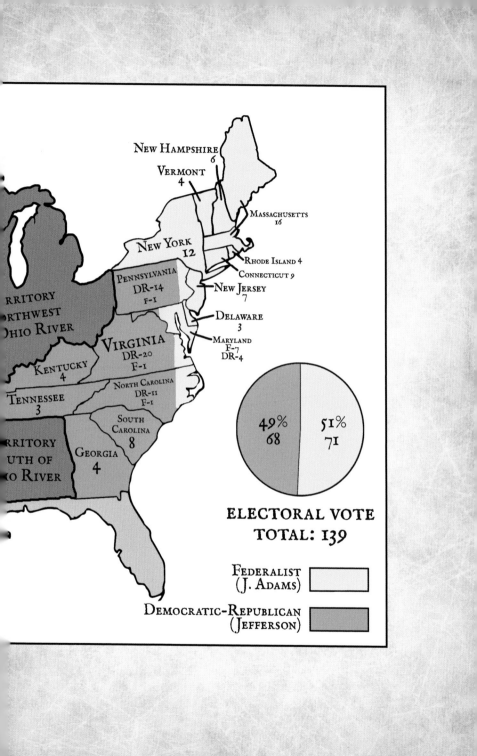

NEW HAMPSHIRE
6

VERMONT
4

MASSACHUSETTS
16

NEW YORK
12

RHODE ISLAND 4

CONNECTICUT 9

PENNSYLVANIA
DR-14
F-1

NEW JERSEY
7

TERRITORY
NORTHWEST
OHIO RIVER

DELAWARE
3

MARYLAND
F-7
DR-4

VIRGINIA
DR-20
F-1

KENTUCKY
4

NORTH CAROLINA
DR-11
F-1

TENNESSEE
3

SOUTH
CAROLINA
8

TERRITORY
SOUTH OF
OHIO RIVER

GEORGIA
4

49%
68

51%
71

**ELECTORAL VOTE
TOTAL: 139**

FEDERALIST
(J. ADAMS)

DEMOCRATIC-REPUBLICAN
(JEFFERSON)

asked, "Freedom, do you have any questions we could answer? I know you have a creative young mind, eager for knowledge, and we are at your disposal."

Freedom sat up in her chair, paused, and then said in a soft voice, "Um, this may be a dumb question, but my friend is trying to get elected president of our school. What are the best things he can do to win?"

Mrs. Adams looked at Freedom kindly and said, "That is not a dumb question at all. I am absolutely thrilled to hear your friend is interested in serving at a young age. John?" She lightly elbowed the President, who nodded while taking a bite of biscuit.

President Adams lit up. "Oh, I love this. There are so many things that go into an election, but if I had to choose a few . . . Let's see, I think it would be three things. First, to pick a strategy to win; second, to have faith in your own strategy; and third, to stick with it even when the odds are against you. I won the election last year by only three votes. There were people who tried every trick in the book, but we were strong in our principles, and succeeded."

The President paused and looked at his wife tenderly. "What would you recommend, Mrs. Adams? What advice would you give to the future president of Freedom's school?"

Mrs. Adams crinkled her brow and said, "Well, of course you need some basics to be a strong candidate: loyalty, caring for family, an education on all aspects of the election, and an ability to do many different projects at once."

Freedom nodded sincerely.

"And, once you have these, I believe the most important strategy in an election is to listen closely to those who have not previously been heard. If you have a strong team, they will help you in this task. It is something that is easy to forget in the midst of an election, but I believe it is vital."

"Thank you so much, President and Mrs. Adams," Freedom said gently. "I will be sure to tell my friend everything you said. I will write it all in his playbook."

Right as she said that, it dawned on me. The notebook was in Liberty's saddlebag and Liberty was in the water. *Oh no*, I thought.

During a pause in conversation, I decided to check on Liberty. Freedom and I excused ourselves, saying that we were going to get a notebook from our horse's saddlebag.

As we left the tavern we found Liberty dripping wet on the road.

Seeing us coming, Liberty said, "So I have an explanation. I was a little dusty so I wanted to take a quick bath. Can you blame me? I don't want to be mistaken for a dust ball. That would be sad."

Freedom giggled and took out the playbook. It was a little wet but not soaked due to the liner of the saddlebag.

I patted Liberty on the side and said, "I am going to pop inside to ask where the nearest five-star hotel and platinum horse spa are located."

Liberty looked pleased until he realized I was joking, then he mumbled, "Not funny, Revere, not funny at all."

I couldn't help but laugh as Freedom and I returned to the tavern.

The President pulled out his pocket watch and said, "I am afraid to say, we really must be going."

Mrs. Adams agreed to leave and we stood. On the way out of the tavern, she said, "One more thing your friend must remember—wear a suit of armor. Well, not a real one," she said laughing. "But honestly, the closer your friend gets to the election, the more things will become difficult for him. No matter how many negative things are said, he cannot let it ruin his plan for the country—I mean school."

"I think I understand," said Freedom. She quickly scribbled *armor* and added *Elizabeth* in Cam's playbook.

Mrs. Adams said firmly, "There will be people who will attack your friend. Maybe they already have. And the closer he is to victory the harder the attacks will be. Do not let it affect your plan. One thing that surprised us a little about the presidency is the awful nature of the newspapers. They have attacked John brutally and are attempting to destroy his good name, and this after years of service to the country, including his time during the Revolutionary War. It is a disgrace."

Freedom looked at Mrs. Adams and said softly, "Sometimes when people are making fun of you, you get stronger because you have to."

"Brilliant, Freedom, and very true," President Adams agreed. "Mrs. Adams and I are far stronger together because of the relentless attacks by the newspapers."

We thanked President and Mrs. Adams for their time and the wonderful meal.

At that, we parted ways. The President and Mrs. Adams entered his carriage for Philadelphia and we gathered Liberty to find a place to open the portal.

On the words *"Rush, rush, rushing from history,"* the portal magically appeared. Before I could blink, we were crossing through the purple and yellow sparkles back to modern day.

John Adams, the second president of the United States, was born here. You can still visit his early home at the Adams National Historical Park.

This Abigail Adams coin was made by the U.S. Mint. The image on the back portrays her famous letter, "Remember the Ladies."

Chapter 9

The next morning, Cam and Tommy drank hot chocolate and stared at Freedom like she was telling a ghost story.

"And then, at the last second, Mr. Revere pulled me away from the charging horses pulling the second carriage. And do you know who was inside?" Freedom paused for dramatic effect and then nodded at Liberty.

"Da-da-dum," Liberty said.

Freedom exclaimed loudly, "It was the President's wife, Abigail Adams!"

"No way," said Tommy. "That's crazy."

"Wait," said Cam. "You're saying President John Adams and his wife, Abigail Adams, were racing each other in carriages to see who could get to the President's House first?"

"Wow," said Tommy. "I wonder how much horsepower they had in the carriages—get it? They were pulled by horses."

"Not your best, Tommy, not your best," Liberty teased.

Freedom shook her head. "No, it is because they were so in love they were racing *to* each other."

Cam and Tommy let out a joint sarcastic "Awwww."

"Oh, whatever, guys," Freedom said. "I bet you and your girlfriend Elizabeth would love a carriage ride, Tommy."

"Yuck," he replied, mock-trembling.

"Honestly, Mrs. Adams was really incredible, like a war reporter and everything," Freedom said.

"She sounds really cool. But did you learn anything to help with my election?" Cam said eagerly.

Freedom pulled the playbook from Liberty's saddlebag. "Actually, I have some good stuff for Team Cam," she said, opening the notebook. "By the way, your playbook almost got soaked when Liberty took a bath. But don't worry, I saved it."

"Hey, Cam, you would have been one unhappy Cam-per," Tommy joked, looking around the table. "C'mon, Liberty, you know that was funny."

Liberty shook his head. "Maybe I'll think it's funny Tommy-orrow." He winked and shook his body happily.

"Honestly, guys, that playbook has all of my election notes. I'm not sure what I would do without it," Cam said, grabbing the notebook from the center of the table and hugging it.

"Thank goodness for saddlebag liners," I said, looking at Liberty.

"So what did you find out?" Cam asked as he started thumbing through the pages.

"Check this out," Freedom said as she slipped the notebook out of Cam's hands and opened it. "President and Mrs. Adams talked a lot. They were really great partners and obviously really appreciated each other." Freedom paused to think for a moment. "One thing Mrs. Adams said was you have to wear a suit of armor and not let anyone or anything get you off of your strategy. She said the newspapers were really mean to her husband but they couldn't let that get to them."

"That is similar to what George Washington advised, remember?" I said. "I think you have ten plays so far in the playbook. This can be play eleven: *Develop armor against criticism.*"

Cam nodded. He took the notebook from Freedom and added a note, and placed it back on the center of the table.

I continued, "As Freedom said, the Adamses were attacked in the newspapers and by their competition. This happens a lot nowadays, too, in our national election. As we have the First Amendment's freedom of speech and press, campaigns can become quite hostile at times. The current presidential candidates must rise above all of the noise and stick to their plan. You could say they all need a suit of armor."

Tommy pulled a football out of his backpack. "Stand up, Cam. I want you to pretend this football is a dumb comment from Elizabeth."

Cam stood up and nodded. "Okay, what do I do?"

"You have to stand up straight like a goalpost and let the football bounce off of you."

Cam clenched his fists at his sides. "I'm ready." He focused on Tommy.

In a high-pitched voice, Tommy said, "Hey, Cam, I'm going to win student body president because you are a poo-poo head." He threw the football and it hit Cam square in the chest. He was only a couple of feet away so it couldn't have hurt too much.

I couldn't tell if Cam was laughing, grunting, or both. Either

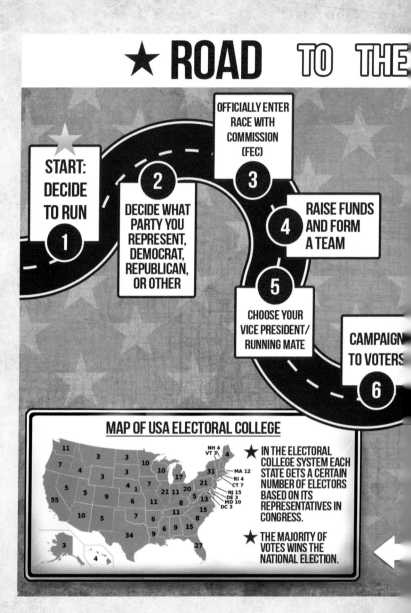

★ ROAD TO THE

START: DECIDE TO RUN ①

2 **DECIDE WHAT PARTY YOU REPRESENT, DEMOCRAT, REPUBLICAN, OR OTHER**

OFFICIALLY ENTER RACE WITH COMMISSION (FEC) **3**

RAISE FUNDS AND FORM A TEAM **4**

5 **CHOOSE YOUR VICE PRESIDENT/ RUNNING MATE**

CAMPAIGN TO VOTERS **6**

MAP OF USA ELECTORAL COLLEGE

★ IN THE ELECTORAL COLLEGE SYSTEM EACH STATE GETS A CERTAIN NUMBER OF ELECTORS BASED ON ITS REPRESENTATIVES IN CONGRESS.

★ THE MAJORITY OF VOTES WINS THE NATIONAL ELECTION.

Here are the steps to become president
of the United States. Extra credit:
what is the Electoral College?

PRESIDENCY ★

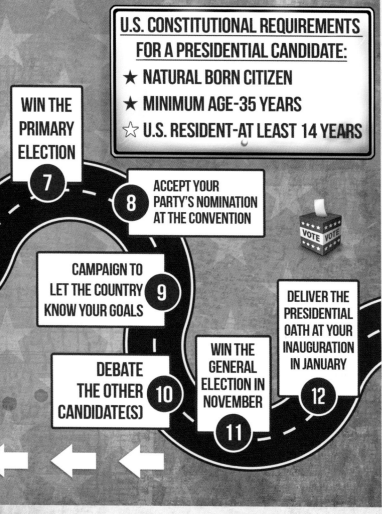

U.S. CONSTITUTIONAL REQUIREMENTS FOR A PRESIDENTIAL CANDIDATE:
- ★ NATURAL BORN CITIZEN
- ★ MINIMUM AGE-35 YEARS
- ☆ U.S. RESIDENT-AT LEAST 14 YEARS

WIN THE PRIMARY ELECTION 7

ACCEPT YOUR PARTY'S NOMINATION AT THE CONVENTION 8

CAMPAIGN TO LET THE COUNTRY KNOW YOUR GOALS 9

DEBATE THE OTHER CANDIDATE(S) 10

WIN THE GENERAL ELECTION IN NOVEMBER 11

DELIVER THE PRESIDENTIAL OATH AT YOUR INAUGURATION IN JANUARY 12

VOTE VOTE

way, the ball bounced off his chest. He raised his hands in the air and said, "I've got armor on, oh yeah! You can't touch this!"

Liberty snorted, laughing.

Freedom pulled the playbook closer to her, looked at her notes, and said, "President and Mrs. Adams also said it's really important to reach as many people as possible and pay attention to the people who don't normally have a voice."

"Who doesn't have a voice?" Cam asked.

I said, "I think Mrs. Adams was basically saying the same thing that Congressman Joseph said. Instead of just focusing on 'cool' kids like Elizabeth does, reach out to as many students as possible. Visit the different sports groups, clubs, and other places students meet. I think you have this in your notebook as play number ten."

"I bet it would have been a lot easier for the Adamses to tell people about their views if they had social media back in the day," said Freedom.

"Yeah, how cool would it be to see President Adams's Facebook page from the 1800s, right, Mr. Revere?" Tommy joked.

As two middle-school-aged girls passed our table, Cam stood up and proudly announced, "President Cam is a man of the people! I will preserve, protect, and defend the Constitution of the United States of America." He smiled and bowed like George Washington at his inauguration.

The girls looked at Cam and giggled as they walked by faster. One was wearing a jacket with "USA" written on the back. She waved and smiled at Cam.

We all smiled.

Tommy laughed and nudged Cam. "I think you have one vote already."

Freedom clapped. "Well done, President Cam!"

We spent the next few minutes talking through Cam's election strategy. Before I knew it, the alarm on my watch went off. It was time for class.

About a week later, in our afternoon American Adventurers meeting, Cam was full of energy. He bounced around the room as if he were warming up for a basketball game. I was about to ask him to take his seat, when he plopped into a chair next to Tommy and whispered something in his ear. They both laughed and gave each other a high five.

Right then, a voice came over the loudspeaker.

"If there are any Manchester Middle School students still here, this is your future student body president, Elizabeth. Me and the rest of the cheerleaders are looking for some really cool volunteers to help with my election campaign. If you are not cool, don't even bother to apply. Yo, we put the cool in school, unlike some people. Yeah, Cameron, that's you."

Cam's face was unreadable. His eyes were serious and focused.

Elizabeth continued over the loudspeaker, "Cool kids, meet us at the gym tomorrow morning before school to sign up. Free Popsicles for everyone who joins Team Cool. Bye for now." The loudspeaker wailed as she turned it off.

After that interruption, it took a bit to refocus. I asked everyone to show me how well they were doing with their handshake. Soon everyone was laughing, and we were able to continue our game.

As soon as the club meeting was over I waved Cam, Tommy, and Freedom over to my desk. The rest of the students left the classroom.

"How's that armor holding up, Cam?" I asked.

"I think it has a big dent in it after Elizabeth's announcement, but I'll survive."

He gave me a half smile.

"Good for you, Cam. I'm really proud of you. If you guys can give me just a few minutes, I'm thinking through an idea," I said.

"Sure thing, Mr. Revere. We have plenty of strategy stuff to talk about," Freedom replied.

I brainstormed for a few minutes and it dawned on me. We had already learned a great deal from Washington and Adams for Cam's election playbook. But he still didn't have his speech fully written. I knew that all the candidates' speeches, including Cam's, were scheduled for three days away.

"Okay, guys, I just thought of something that should work," I said, clapping my hands together. "Cam, you have your big speech coming up, right?"

Cam nodded.

"We have one big advantage that Elizabeth doesn't," I said.

"What is it, Mr. Revere? She has lots of things going for her, including the intercom," replied Cam.

"How about we time-travel back to meet one of the greatest writers of all time, Thomas Jefferson? He was brilliant, loved to read, and was the main author of the Declaration of Independence. He was the third President of the United States, after John Adams."

"Boo-ya! Now we're talking!" exclaimed Cam.

Tommy smiled and said, "I'm not missing this one. I'm definitely in. Plus he has my name, so I have to go." He low-fived Cam.

"What about football practice?" said Freedom.

"Not today, because we won our game yesterday," Tommy replied.

"Way to go on the win. Can I go, Mr. Revere?" Freedom asked.

"Of course. It sounds like we're all going. Let's go find Liberty."

Suddenly, Liberty appeared inside the classroom. "I'm already here, Captain, ready for my orders. And I know you're all wondering why I'm inside the school. Lucky for you I heard Elizabeth's voice over the loudspeaker and rushed in as fast as horsily possible, ready to take out Eliza-Vader. You know, like in Darth Vader, but his evil twin sister."

Where does he come up with this stuff? I thought. "All right, everyone. This will work well, I think. Grab your colonial clothes out of Liberty's saddlebag and I'll move these desks to the side so we can time-jump."

Once we were ready, I had Tommy and Freedom ride Liberty while Cam and I followed behind on foot. I gave Liberty the year and place I wanted to travel to and Liberty said, *"Rush, rush, rushing to history!"* The portal opened and we jumped through the spinning purple and gold swirl.

We landed in the middle of the woods. In fact there were so many trees I was a bit disoriented. Everywhere we turned there were brown and white trees with green leaves and branches. At our feet there was moss, dirt, and bushes. I looked for a path but couldn't find one.

"Are you sure we landed in the right place, Liberty? I don't see President Jefferson's house or for that matter any people at all. In fact, this does not look like the city of Washington in 1803 that I read about," I said.

"Hold on, let me concentrate for a second," Liberty replied, closing his eyes. He opened them and said, "Okay, okay, got it. My inner GPS tells me the President's House is in that direction. Not too far from here, past those trees." He pointed his nose behind me, past my left shoulder.

"Perfect," I said. "Come on, guys, follow me." I turned to walk toward the President's House with Cam following. Tommy and Freedom were still on Liberty's back.

In less than a minute we came to the edge of the woods. In front of us was the President's House that would later be called the White House. Here in 1803, it looked like a construction site, with workers milling about, and carriages coming and going. There were no cars zipping past or horns honking.

"Before we leave the woods let me fill you in a bit about President Thomas Jefferson," I said. "He was originally from Virginia and was close friends with James Madison. Remember we met James Madison, who was known as the Father of the Constitution, at the Constitutional Convention in 1787?"

"That was right before the crazy French guy chased us through the streets of Philadelphia, remember that?" Tommy laughed.

"And of course the writing of the Constitution," I said, winking.

"Oh yeah, that too."

"Anyway, Thomas Jefferson served as a member of the Virginia House of Delegates, where he fought for religious freedom. He became the governor of Virginia and escaped from British soldiers during the Revolutionary War. He later went overseas as minister to France, and secretary of state under George Washington. That is the main representative of the president for relationships with other countries. He lost to John Adams in the election of 1796 and became vice president. Get this, back then, the loser became the vice president. Cam, can you imagine Elizabeth as your vice president?"

Tommy said, "That's crazy. Why would you do all that work running for president just to become vice president. Weird."

Cam crossed his arms and said, "No way. No way would Elizabeth be my vice president."

I smiled and continued: "Thomas Jefferson ran again for president in 1800 and this time he won the election and became—"

Liberty interrupted. "Look at the bird's nest up in that tree. Can you hear the chirping? Oh, look, I see a little bird head poking out from the side."

"Liberty, this is a history trip, not a—"

"Oh, no, the nest is tipping. I think it might fall to the ground," said Liberty, deeply concerned.

I sighed. "Let me stand on your saddle and see if I can stabilize the nest."

Balancing on Liberty's saddle I reached up toward the nest, when suddenly the nest fell. Liberty darted forward just in time and caught the nest on his nose. But the saddle slipped out from under my feet. I grasped the nearest branch and hung four feet off the ground. I felt like I was trying to do the monkey bars on the playground.

"Mr. Revere, are you okay?" asked Tommy, trying to help.

"Yes, I'm just hanging around," I joked.

I noticed the ground wasn't too far down so I released my grip and fell with a thud. I slipped on the slick leaves and fell on my rump. *Classic, Revere, classic*, I thought. As I got up and brushed myself off I found myself face-to-face with a dark brown horse that I had never seen before. *You're not Liberty*, I thought. I looked up and saw a man slouched in the saddle. He was very tall, with reddish hair and long arms and legs. His nose jutted out from his high cheekbones and he wore his hair long and tucked back like George Washington. He held the horse's reins tight and wore a brown jacket and breeches.

"Do you need assistance, sir?" the man asked in a soft voice. He dismounted and approached me.

"I'm fine. Just a little clumsy," I replied. "I am getting a little old for jumping from trees, I am afraid."

"May I inquire as to your name?" asked the red-haired gentleman. He towered over Tommy.

I was about to reply, when Tommy said, "My name is Tommy, and my friends Cam and Freedom are over there. We're students from Manchester Middle School."

"Well, of course, students," the man said. "How wonderful. I do not recognize that school name—'Manchester Middle,' where is that?" Before we could answer he continued, "It is always a pleasure to meet those in search of an education. And the woods are a wonderful place for scientific adventure."

I looked closely at the man and a memory stirred.

Just then, Freedom ran over and said, "Mr. Revere, we have to help this little bird. Its nest fell out of a tree but Liberty caught it just in time."

Sure enough, Liberty was standing motionless with the bird nest on his nose. If I thought of being mad at Liberty for pulling the saddle out from under me, it evaporated immediately. Cam was close by and we all leaned over to see a tiny bluebird still in its nest. It was chirping and looked to have hurt its wing in the fall.

"How interesting," said the red-haired man. "You say the horse saved this bird? You have a very smart horse."

Liberty looked down with half-closed eyes like a wise professor, and lowered the bird and nest gently to the ground.

The man pulled out a scarf. "Young lady, please take this kerchief and cover the bird and the nest. My house is right over there. We will take it there for its recovery. Do not touch the bird with your hands, as you may harm it."

Freedom clutched the handkerchief, bird, and nest and we all walked out of the woods.

All of a sudden, it dawned on me—the house the man was speaking about was the President's House. We were speaking with the president of the United States, Thomas Jefferson.

"Mr. President," I said apologetically, "I am so sorry for bothering you. I know you must be very busy. I cannot believe I did not immediately recognize you, sir. I was a bit dazed after my fall from the tree. My name is Rush Revere and these are my students."

Thomas Jefferson laughed and turned to shake my hand with great energy. "It is no problem at all. I ride my horse daily. It is nice to remove myself from the rigors of office for a while. I consider this a very entertaining way to spend the afternoon, made more entertaining on having met such a lovely group of new friends."

The crew all looked at me wide-eyed once they realized with whom we were speaking.

"Very good, Freedom. You are doing splendidly," President Jefferson said. "Carry the bird carefully, as this path can be a little tricky."

"I will," Freedom replied.

Mr. Jefferson then mounted his horse and rode slightly ahead of us. He said, "I will lead the way. Just follow along right behind."

Do you know who the man is at the center of this picture?
He liked to ride horses in the afternoon.

As we walked, Liberty whispered to me, "I'm sorry about what happened back there. My instincts took over. I'm just glad you're okay."

"No harm done," I said smiling. "I'm always happy to go out on a *limb* for these adventures."

Liberty chuckled. "Good one, Revere."

As we walked I thought about how amazing it was that the President could ride alone in the woods near his home. In modern day that wouldn't be possible because there would be a team of Secret Service members following the President everywhere he went, and it would be nearly impossible to speak to the President.

After a few minutes we arrived at the President's House. Despite the construction, it was beautiful up close. The building looked similar to the modern White House, with two stories and large windows, but it was unfinished. On the grounds there were pieces of wood and brick piled up everywhere.

President Jefferson dismounted his horse and a young boy of about fifteen years old took the reins. Then another boy grabbed Liberty's reins and led him off. He looked happy to go. No doubt he'd be fed.

We continued to follow Thomas Jefferson, who was leading us into his house—the White House!

As we entered I looked around and was amazed to walk into a room that looked like a museum. On the walls there were historical artifacts along with animals of all kinds, maps, and statues. In the middle of the room were large columns. There were almost too many things to view at one time, including two birdcages with real birds in them.

Freedom held the nest with the injured bird close as she

walked through the center of the room. Cam and Tommy stood with their mouths open, looking at all the different items. It was clear that President Jefferson loved science, and enjoyed the study of animals, including birds.

"Freedom, please place the bird over there," said Jefferson, pointing to an empty birdcage. "Let's find out what kind of bird it is." No one else was in the house and everything seemed quiet. There were books everywhere.

President Jefferson pointed to a caged bird with a yellow chest and black and white body. He spoke with Freedom for quite a while about its coloring and the regions where it lived. President Jefferson spoke about nurturing it back to health and releasing it again to the wild. At one point while we watched, he walked up to a cage in the corner of the room and released a small bird with a red head, which flew happily around the room.

All of a sudden, there was a knock on the door.

"Enter," the President called out.

A man came racing into the room. "Mr. President, Napoleon and the French have agreed to the purchase of the Louisiana Territory!" the man said excitedly, nearly out of breath.

"Excellent, for what price?" the President asked in a serious tone.

"For fifteen million dollars, Mr. President, approximately three cents per acre. The French have sold over eight hundred thousand square miles of land to us."

President Jefferson's face lit up into a wide smile. With energy he said, "This is brilliant news. Soon we will begin to explore these lands and bring back scientific knowledge that will greatly benefit our people."

"That is wonderful news, Mr. President," I said.

"Thank you, Mr. Revere. I need to go and speak with my secretary, Mr. Meriwether Lewis, about it. I expect there will be an expedition to Louisiana soon."

Cam, Tommy, and Freedom stared intently at the President.

"Freedom, I will return very soon to make sure this bird is well cared for," the President added as he left the room. "Please look around at the artifacts for a few moments while I discuss these matters of state. Now, if you will excuse me . . ."

We all smiled and began politely touring the room. "I can't believe we are here. I mean, we're actually in the President's House just kinda hangin' out," Cam said, eyes wide.

Tommy laughed and said, "I know, right? *So what did you guys do today? Oh, well, we hung out with President Jefferson and his birds. You know, the usual.*"

We all started chortling like when you hear a joke in a library but can't laugh out loud.

"Fifteen million dollars sounds like a lot of coin. Was Jefferson happy with the deal?" Tommy asked.

I smiled. "Yes, because the Louisiana Purchase was one of the most important decisions by a president in American history. It doubled the size of the country." I walked over to a map of North America on Jefferson's wall. "Come look here."

The crew walked closer to the map.

"This is Louisiana and here is the area of the original thirteen colonies. By purchasing this land, Thomas Jefferson removed the French, who could have easily become hostile and taken over the colonies. This decision to make this historic purchase opened the door to westward expansion so we could eventually have states like California."

"That's awesome!" said Cam.

Modern-day White House.

President's House in 1807.

After a few minutes, President Jefferson returned, apologizing for being forced to leave us.

"No problem whatsoever. We are thrilled to meet you and honored to spend even a moment here," I said.

"Now, Freedom, where were we?" the President asked as he walked over to the tiny bluebird and put his face very close to its eye.

"Mr. President, your time is so valuable and we are so thankful for it. Would you be so kind as to answer a question for my students?"

"By all means," President Jefferson replied.

"Is there something in particular you would say is the most important part of being president?" I asked.

President Jefferson thought for a moment. He looked at me and carefully replied, "My first and only focus is what will be best for the people of our country. During the sacrifices of the Revolution, we fought for freedom from the abuses of the King. As president it is my duty to ensure that these freedoms are maintained. There are always those who attempt to limit the rights of the people and I am strict in following the words of the Constitution. Even if I strongly believe in doing something, I must first think what is best for the American people. My role is to serve the people, not the other way around."

Swept up in the moment, I wanted to tell the President how much we celebrate and remember him and his words in modern day. How every child reads his Declaration of Independence, and how the words are used to protect the rights of people around the world. But then I remembered it was still 1803, and he would not understand what I meant. So instead I simply said, "Your words will live on forever, Mr. President."

"Why, thank you, Mr. Revere. That is most kind. You should also know that the furtherance of education of young people is one of my greatest goals in life. So I thank you for your work as a teacher."

I bowed my head slightly, in response to his kind words.

Cam didn't move a muscle while the President spoke. He was focused on every word.

The President looked again at the injured bird, and then back to us. "At times, it gets a little too quiet here even for my work, and even a bit lonely. It is a pleasure to speak with you."

At that moment, Cam summoned up the courage to say, "Mr. President, I know you are busy, but is it okay if I ask you another question?"

President Jefferson looked up and over at Cam. "Why, of course, young man. I would be most happy to answer, if I can."

Cam cleared his throat as if he were a reporter in the modern-day White House Briefing Room and asked, "Mr. President, how did you write the Declaration of Independence? I have to do a speech at school for my election soon, and I am having trouble finding the right words."

"That is a splendid question," President Jefferson replied. "Which part is the most difficult for you?"

"Um, I think it is just I have so many ideas, but I don't know how to write them so that people understand. Like I want to have more school spirit but I can't just say, *I will give you more school spirit.* It's hard."

The President leaned up against a desk and looked attentively at Cam. "Ah, now I understand, yes, of course. The first step is that you must work diligently. I spent the summer of 1776 working on the Declaration of Independence with Benjamin

Franklin and John Adams, among others. During that time, we were at war with the British." The President looked around the room at all of us. "I sat at my desk and wrote every day, until the words were exactly as I wished them to be. In your case, time is limited, but it is still important to make sure you make the effort to create something you can be proud of, no matter the result of the election."

"I will work really hard, Mr. President. But how do I know what to write?"

"Have you spoken with students around your school, and asked them what they want?"

"Yes, I tried to talk to everyone I could. They had lots of ideas, things that they thought we could do better at school."

"Then that is your answer. That is what you will write. When I wrote the Declaration of Independence, my simple objective was to list the reasons for our separation from the King and Great Britain, placing before mankind the common sense of the subject."

Cam looked confused. "I'm sorry I don't really understand, sir."

"It is complex, I understand, Cam. I simply mean that you should write clearly, and list the exact ways you want to help the school and other students. People can sense if you are not being truthful, so aim to prove to them that you are the best leader to serve them. Then ask for their support."

"Thank you, Mr. President."

"Good, young man. So, now you are ready with the basics. You will work hard and have the details you gathered from your classmates to use in your speech. If you are truthful, the audience will begin to trust you, and will begin to listen to your words. Now comes the difficult part."

The President rose and walked around the room. He took a deep breath as he paced. When he turned to us, his eyes had a faraway look. He said, "I remember that summer, when I was writing the Declaration of Independence. Every night I would sleep in the room across from my small wooden desk, and when I arose, I saw the pages in front of me. The more I tried to put the words together and form a clear argument, the more lost I became. I was tied in knots, pulling one and pushing another. Finally, after one late night, a ray of sunlight hit the page in a particular way. I sat at the desk and wrote in the warmth of the light."

"What did you write, Mr. President?" Cam said quietly.

"I wrote the first draft of the words that later became, *We hold these truths to be self-evident, that all men are created equal, that they are endowed by their Creator with certain unalienable Rights, that among these are Life, Liberty and the pursuit of Happiness.*" His face was full of a peaceful humility, but his hands were gesturing a story of their own. His fingers moved with gentleness.

"Wow, that is amazing. Like everyone knows those words. Mr. Revere had me memorize them. That is really cool that you wrote that."

The President appeared pleased to share this moment with Cam.

"I appreciate the compliment, but my purpose in sharing the moment of writing those words is that they did not come from my love of science and philosophy. They came from somewhere else that I cannot easily describe—perhaps we could call it *inspiration*. And that is what you need to find for your speech."

"How do I find that?" Cam asked, perplexed.

Thomas Jefferson slept in a bed near his desk while writing
the Declaration of Independence. Do you remember what advice
he gave Cam about writing his speech?

"That is the trick!" Thomas Jefferson smiled widely. When he looked up his eyes were full of such energy, and such kindness, that anything seemed possible. "I do not know where it comes from but you know when it happens. Begin with hard work and a good argument, then think of the best way to connect with your audience. When you feel it in your chest, you know you have something. I am sorry if that is not clear, but it is the best way to describe it."

"*Inspiration?*" Cam mused.

"That's right, and perhaps it comes from somewhere beyond ourselves that we do not understand. Perhaps it is our Lord, I do not know. That is why you must have faith."

Right then, another man entered the room with urgent business. The President apologized, but I did not want to overstay our welcome. We thanked him profusely for his time. Freedom said a special goodbye to her little bird friend and wished it well.

We exited in the same direction that we had entered.

"I think President Jefferson is one of the nicest people I have ever met in my whole life," Freedom said. "He is the president of the United States and he spent so much time listening to us and giving us advice. I just can't believe it."

"I want to be a leader just like him," Cam said. "No matter what, I always want to listen to people, and not ignore them. I want them to trust me."

"Totally," said Tommy.

"I think we have a new play for your playbook when we get back," I said. "How about we call it play twelve: *Inspire people in your words and actions.*"

"I hope the little birdie will be okay," Freedom said, looking back. "But I think President Jefferson will take care of him."

Thomas Jefferson served as the third president of the United States from March 4, 1801, until March 4, 1809. Can you name a few of his leadership qualities?

I was so proud of my students.

As we walked outside, I caught a glimpse of Liberty in the distance. The stable hands had finished brushing him and had just placed his saddle on his back. He looked positively relaxed and seemed to be chatting happily with the other horses. Thanking the boys, I grabbed Liberty by the reins and walked back toward the woods.

"We really should schedule a spa treatment like the one I just had for every history field trip," Liberty said, relaxed. "Let's be honest, I'm a very hardworking horse with sore muscles."

"I'm glad you enjoyed yourself," I said. "But it's time we get back to modern day. Tomorrow is the big election for Cam."

We found a quiet area and Liberty said, *"Rush, rush, rushing from history!"*

We flew forward in time back to modern day.

Chapter 10

A few days later, I woke to the sound of hooves clicking on pavement. I tried to keep my eyes closed awhile longer, but as my alarm chimed I could hear banging outside. *Liberty*, I thought. I quickly got out of bed and got dressed.

"Liberty!" I called out as I opened the front door. "What are you doing?"

There was Liberty wearing a formal yellow and white striped tie. Large white headphones were balanced over his large ears. He kept pacing back and forth. Realizing he couldn't hear me, I walked closer to get his attention.

"Good morning," I mouthed.

"Oh, hello, Revere." Liberty shook his large headphones loose.

"You are making quite a ruckus out here. May I ask what you're doing?"

"I decided to dress up for the occasion. I hope you don't mind that I borrowed one of your ties. And, of course, I had to pump myself up with some music. You know, to get in the zone and be prepared. This is the big day, Revere." Liberty looked serious. "Did you forget that it's Cam's speech day?"

Liberty was like an Olympic athlete getting ready before the big race. I couldn't help but laugh. "Of course I didn't forget."

"And what exactly is so funny?" Liberty asked, squinting his eyes.

"Oh nothing," I replied, giving him a fresh red apple. "I just wasn't prepared for a giant rooster wake-me-up at five A.M."

"I can't be a sleepyhead today, Revere. I am Cam's campaign advisor, and I have a few last-minute tips to give him."

"Sounds good. I must say I am a little nervous for Cam. I hope he does well."

"Me too," Liberty agreed.

We finished gathering our belongings and left the house on the way to Manchester Middle School. The whole way we spoke about what Cam might say in his speech.

As soon as we reached the school, Cam, Tommy, and Freedom came rushing up to us. They were breathing heavily.

"Mr. Revere, we saw where Cam and Elizabeth are going to give their speeches," Freedom said. "All the other candidates for student body president dropped out, so it's down to them."

Tommy added, "Yeah, it will be right at the front of the auditorium. There is a wood podium thing at the front of the room."

"Nice tie," Cam said, looking at Liberty. "We kinda match." Cam wore a light tan jacket and purple striped tie.

Liberty nodded proudly.

"You look great, Cam," I said. "Very presidential. How do you feel? Are you feeling confident? A little nervous? Do you have your speech ready?"

"Mr. Revere, it's like we're back in the White House Briefing Room and you are a reporter." Cam smiled brightly. "Just kidding. I'm doing great. I studied my playbook nonstop last night and this morning. I looked at the stuff Thomas Jefferson said about writing a great speech, and I think I came up with a really good one."

I smiled, feeling relieved. "Well done, Cam, that is super."

"Can I see your playbook, Cam?" Freedom asked. "I want to remember what I wrote about Mrs. Adams. She's definitely my favorite First Lady."

"Sure!" Cam exclaimed. He slipped his backpack off his back, and opened the flap. He searched through several layers of books and papers. Then he unzipped a front pocket, searching with greater energy. A look of panic flashed on his face. "Where's my playbook?" Cam's eyes darted from Tommy to Freedom and back to Tommy.

"It's not in your bag?" Tommy asked.

"No," Cam said seriously. "Dude, not a funny prank. What did you do with it?"

Tommy shrugged. "I wouldn't do that, man; it's your big day."

Cam looked again through his backpack. "It's not here."

Liberty leaned over the bag. "Oh no, that happens to me all the time. It is the worst! Where do you think you left it?"

Cam shook his head. "I don't know." His shoulders sank.

"Okay, let's trace your steps," I said. "Where were you right before here?"

"We were all by our lockers," Freedom replied.

"Did you go anywhere after that?" Liberty asked. "Maybe the cafeteria for a snack? That happens, you know."

"No," Cam said, scrunching his eyebrows. Then he paused and said, "Well, I went to the bathroom 'cause I had to fix my tie in the mirror. But I didn't take my bag or my other things with me. I had a few other books and some campaign stuff."

"You didn't take your things with you?" Freedom asked, as if she had thought of something. "Where did you leave the other stuff?"

"Nowhere. I just left it all by the lockers when I went to the bathroom for like two minutes," Cam replied.

"Maybe your playbook is still there!" Tommy yelled as he started running toward the school entrance. "I'll go look!"

"Mr. Revere, this is really bad. The speech is in a few hours and the notebook has all the stuff I learned from Congressman Joseph and everybody from history and my whole speech." Cam looked at me with worried eyes.

I put my hand on Cam's shoulder. "I understand, buddy. But you already have everything you need to say in your head. You wrote a good speech, you prepared well, you know what you are going to say, and you practiced a lot. And you learned from George Washington how to deal with tough situations, so I think you are okay even if you don't find it."

"Yes, you got this, President Cam. Keep focused," Liberty said. "Also, have something to eat right before you go on to keep your energy up. Maybe you should stick a carrot in your front pocket. You know, just in case. And think good thoughts."

Cam nodded his head slowly, but uncertainly.

"We'd better go to class," Freedom said, tugging on Cam's jacket. They both turned and started walking.

"Good luck, Cam!" Liberty shouted.

"Yes, good luck, Cam," I added. "See you inside a little later."

Liberty and I planned to run a few errands before Cam's big speech but Cam's playbook dilemma made it hard to concentrate on anything else.

"Revere, you look a little pale. Are you okay?" Liberty asked.

"Just still nervous for Cam, I guess, or should I say excited. Both worried and excited."

We walked toward the gate to leave the school grounds.

Liberty smiled. "You are starting to sound like me, Captain." He stopped and looked at me with his head slightly tilted. "You know, when I am nervous or excited, a little snack always seems to do the trick. How about we stop by the bagel shop for a bagel, or two, or three?"

"That's a good idea, Liberty. I could use a cup of coffee right now." We turned the corner, heading toward Boston Bagels. "I really hope Tommy found Cam's playbook. I know he can do it without it, but it gives him some confidence."

Liberty agreed. "I hope so, too. Oh man, oh man. Cam never went anywhere without that playbook. He always had his head down studying and making notes. I bet he is really upset. It's like that one time I lost your house keys. Remember that, Revere? But it all worked out once you cleared all the hay out of the stable. Just a few hours and all was good."

I smiled and shook my head. "That *one* time you lost the house keys?" I joked. "I'm pretty sure I'm finding lost keys a lot."

"A lot?" Liberty sighed. "Revere, that's a bit of an exaggeration, don't you think? Once or twice. Well, possibly five times . . . tops. No more than ten, certainly. And not really lost, more like *misplaced*."

I laughed at Liberty's banter. I had to shush him as a woman passed. She stared as we trotted down the bicycle lane. After a few minutes we arrived at Boston Bagels.

"Okay, okay, ten bagels," I said as Liberty stood near our usual table. "But no garlic."

I went inside, bought the bagels and coffee, and turned to exit. Somewhere behind me I heard, "Mr. Revere?"

I turned around and recognized a familiar face. "Good morning, Congressman," I said. "I am sorry. I was lost in my own world there for a second."

"Good morning, Mr. Revere. Not to worry. I am lost in my own world just about every day." He smiled wide and bright. "No campaign meeting this morning?"

"No, today is Cam's big presidential election speech, so he was preparing on his own this morning."

"Fantastic. He will do great! Be sure to tell him I said hello. As they used to say when I was in the Navy, I wish him *fair winds and following seas*."

"I certainly will, thank you, Congressman. I haven't heard that expression in a number of years. Could you remind me what it means exactly so I can share it with Cam?"

"Of course. It is an expression used by sailors to wish someone a smooth and steady voyage. The *fair winds* and the *following seas* push a vessel forward with ease. It is my hope for any sailor or candidate. As we know, it is not always the case."

I felt a sense of calm sweep over me. "Thank you, Congressman. I will be sure to share that with Cam."

Liberty and I took our breakfast to go and ran a few errands before heading back to school.

When we arrived, we waited under the shade of our favorite oak tree to gather our thoughts.

"So when you see Cam, tell him his campaign advisor says to breathe in and breathe out. And don't fidget with his tie. And remember to think about talking to one friend in the crowd to be less nervous," Liberty said, looking straight into my eyes like a coach.

Just then, I heard a beep and looked down at my phone. In all caps a text message from Cam read:

STILL CAN'T FIND PLAYBOOK. WHAT CAN I DO?

I wrote back:

That's OK. You practiced a lot. You know your speech. Remember George Washington. Stay calm and adjust to the changing circumstances.

Cam wrote back:

OK

I said to Liberty, "I'd better head inside. Try not to get into trouble out here, and I'll let you know as soon as I have any news."

"Sounds like a plan. I will be right here with my fingers and toes crossed." He tried to cross his hooves, unsuccessfully.

I laughed and turned to walk toward the front door. As I went up the front steps and pushed open the door, I thought back to the first day I heard Cam talking about his plans to run for student body president.

Near the lockers, I saw Freedom, Tommy, and Cam huddled

together. Cam was leaning in. As I approached I heard a familiar voice.

"Nice tie, Cameron. That outfit is certainly an *interesting* combination," Elizabeth mocked. "Glad you got all nice and dressed up . . . to lose." She was standing with her pack of near-identical girls, all giggling.

"Ignore them," Freedom said.

"Whatever, Elizabeth, why don't you save your jokes for your speech," Cam said, drawing a nod from Tommy.

"Oh, no, I'm gonna save *your* jokes for *my* speech." She whipped something out from behind her back. "By the way, looking for this?" My heart sank. It was Cam's playbook.

Cam crossed his arms and stared at her. Tommy and Freedom stood up straight beside him.

Elizabeth waved the notebook in the air. "Aww, Cam's little *playbook*. Oh, wow, is that George Washington? That is supercool . . . not."

The girls behind her laughed and passed around Cam's book.

"Stop it, guys, c'mon," Tommy said.

Cam's face turned a shade of red.

"Oh, Thomas, you are so sweet and cute. I'll talk to you later. Maybe you can take me to get ice cream?"

"Nope," Tommy said, shaking his head.

"You'll change your mind, my little pumpkin," she cooed. "Oh, and Cam, see you in front of the whole school. Don't choke this time." She and her crew flipped their hair and turned to go. Turning back, she said, "And I'm gonna take this with me. There are some great things in here that everyone should hear about."

Cam took a step toward them and I yelled, "Cam!"

Elizabeth and her twins had disappeared.

Cam looked back at me seriously. "What am I going to do? That playbook had everything in it."

"I know it's hard, but remember what Abigail Adams said. Wear a suit of armor. Don't let Elizabeth get to you no matter what. Also, I saw Congressman Joseph this morning, and he said to wish you *fair winds and following seas*. That means that he hopes your journey will be smooth. . . ."

Before Cam could respond, Principal Sherman's voice came over the loudspeaker and announced, "The student body president election speeches will start in ten minutes. All teachers and students, please make your way to the auditorium."

I tried to encourage Cam as students and teachers filled the hallway. Students were turning to look at Cam as he made his way through the crowd into the auditorium. I walked behind and watched him and his two good friends walk from the shadows into the bright lights.

Students were finding their places in the theater, and all I could hear was chatter. At the front of the room there was a stage and chairs. Elizabeth was speaking with her father, Principal Sherman, near the podium and microphone. Cam went up to the stage and sat on one of two chairs, and Freedom and Tommy sat in the front. I found a place in the sixth row. My chest was thumping.

"Everyone take your seats. Take your seats," Principal Sherman announced from the podium at the center of the stage. "Please be quiet."

The full auditorium settled down and the whole room was quiet. The microphone shrieked, causing Principal Sherman to glare at the man running the sound system.

He continued, "Welcome to the student body presidential

speeches. Everyone, give a round of applause to Elizabeth and Cam, your presidential candidates." The audience clapped, and some hooted.

Principal Sherman continued, "Both Elizabeth and Cam have carefully prepared remarks in order to seek your vote. Remember to listen closely, as you will cast your vote for best student body president tomorrow morning right after the first bell. Keep in mind, the person who wins will be elected to the student council and will make decisions on your behalf." He looked around the room. Teachers and students alike looked up at him. "We did a coin toss a moment ago, and Elizabeth will be going first. Good luck to both candidates."

Cam sat in his suit onstage, slightly slouched, looking serious. I looked around the auditorium and saw, a few rows away, students I recognized sitting together. On the other side of the room, Ed and the band sat with their instruments.

The room was quiet as Elizabeth rose from her seat. She was immaculately dressed in a light blue suit with a matching hairclip. Her usual frown was replaced with a huge smile. She pointed to her friends and waved both arms above her head.

"Ladies and gentlemen, teachers, and fellow students, good afternoon. It is my pleasure to speak to you today. My name is Elizabeth, and I am running for student body president." Her voice had not a hint of nervousness, and every word flowed from her mouth without hesitation. "As everyone knows, I am the head cheerleader at Manchester Middle School. I am a natural leader. Basically, everyone likes me, and I would be the best president this school has ever had."

Cam still wore a serious expression as he looked at her and was now sitting with his arms crossed.

She smiled widely and looked back at Cam. "I also have some great ideas that will put the *cool* in Manchester Middle School. I will tell you about two, since we don't have all day. First, I don't know about you but the school menu can be a bit bland and boring. I would like to have special fun food days like Taco Tuesdays. . . ."

Tommy quickly stood up in the front row, raised his arm, and yelled "Hey!"

The playbook, I thought.

Freedom gently touched Tommy's arm, causing him to sit back down. Principal Sherman shook a finger at Tommy.

Elizabeth looked down toward Tommy and continued with a huge smile. "Second, I think we should have a School Spirit Day where all the cool kids go out into the center of the field and have a huge huddle. The coolest people can win prizes for great outfits. Oh, nothing from last year, though." She winked. Then she did a little mocking wave toward Freedom.

"So, vote for me, Elizabeth, I'll be the best president . . . you'll see."

The crowd clapped politely with the exception of Tommy and Freedom, who sat with arms crossed.

As Elizabeth returned to her seat, Principal Sherman walked to the microphone and said, "Thank you, Elizabeth, for that fine speech. Cameron, please come up."

Cam slowly rose from his seat. His shoulders were slumped and he looked down at the stage. He did not smile as he walked to the podium. He moved the microphone slightly and it wailed, again. He paused. The auditorium was silent but for a few claps.

"Um, hello, everyone. So, my name is uh . . ." Cam began. "I . . . uh." He stopped. Students began looking around as Cam stood silently for a few seconds. He was moving back and forth with his mouth opening and closing.

Oh no, I thought, *not again*. My stomach clenched. I could hear the crowd begin to chatter.

Elizabeth smirked and neatly tucked her hair behind her ears.

A few more seconds passed in silence. Then a minute, then two. Students were whispering, and it sounded like a large collective groan. The cheerleaders were giggling. I could not believe this was happening, after all his hard work!

All of a sudden, a teacher came briskly walking up the aisle toward the front of the auditorium, holding something under her arm. She walked directly over to where Principal Sherman was seated on the stage and spoke with him with her back to the audience.

What is going on? I thought. Cam didn't even have a chance to speak yet. This was not fair. The teacher and principal continued their discussion as Cam looked back at them nervously from the podium. Another minute passed.

Finally, Principal Sherman bounced to his feet, and moved Cam away from the microphone.

Principal Sherman lifted the microphone on the podium higher so he could speak. "I apologize, everyone. I apologize. This is unexpected. . . ."

Cam stood to the side, and Elizabeth smiled widely as Principal Sherman spoke.

"It has come to my attention that someone"—he turned and looked sternly at his daughter—"although we don't yet know who precisely, seems to have taken Cameron's speech notes. We do not condone this behavior at Manchester Middle and will get to the bottom of it." He turned to Cam and handed him the playbook. "I believe this is yours, Cameron."

I heard some of the teachers in the audience gasp. Students were whispering to each other, sounding like a group of bees. The teacher onstage smiled at Cam.

"I am sorry for the delay, everyone. Cam, please continue your speech," Principal Sherman said, motioning for Cam to return to the podium.

Cam moved slowly back to the microphone, standing up straight. He smiled a serious smile. The auditorium returned to near silence.

Softly he began. "Hello, everyone. My name is Cam, and I am running for student body president." There was light applause. Cam looked down at the podium where his playbook rested. He paused, looked up toward Tommy and Freedom. He put a hand on his playbook, but kept it closed.

Cam continued, "I was going to tell you about some of my ideas for fun lunches and School Spirit Day, but it seems like my fellow candidate, Elizabeth, has already done that." Cam looked directly at Elizabeth, then smiled gently at the crowd. Elizabeth laughed, then smiled at the other cheerleaders. Cam glanced at her but pushed through, his voice growing stronger. "Those were good ideas, weren't they, Elizabeth? But, you know what? I've got a lot more ideas like that." The auditorium applauded with more energy.

Cam looked in my direction. "You know, I learned a lot running for president. One of the things I learned is that good leaders cannot give up no matter what their opponents try to do to knock them off their game. No matter how much they bully you, or tease you, no matter how much they make you feel like you're just not cool, you don't have to ever quit. Remember that."

Students in the audience seemed focused on Cam's words. I looked over at Ed and remembered the day Cam protected him from the much bigger Billy the Bully.

Cam was now standing tall as he spoke, looking calmly to the left and right. "Manchester Middle is a great school, but I'd like to make it even better. I have some really cool ideas but, more importantly, I want to hear yours. If you elect me school president, you can all come to me at any time. Ed and the band, you can come to me and tell me what's on your minds. Tommy and the football team, you can come to me and tell me how to make this school even greater. Freedom and the art club, all of you American Adventurers, and you cheerleaders, even you. You can all talk to me at any time. I am here to *serve* you as some very wise friends once told me. I want to use your ideas to make the school better."

Someone yelled, "Go Cam!" and claps and whistles began to come from different corners of the auditorium. Cam was now standing with such poise, he reminded me of George Washington.

"I can't promise all ideas will work, but I will make sure as your president that all your ideas will be heard."

He pointed at the crowd much like a candidate for the national election and repeated, "Your ideas *will . . . be . . . heard!*"

At this, the students burst into loud cheers and applause. Cam paused to flash a wide smile, scanning the crowd with his eyes. Tommy and Freedom stood and cheered, raising their arms above their heads.

As the crowd settled back down, Cam continued, "Tomorrow, please remember to vote for me to serve as your student body president. The C in my name stands for *Cares about you*. You all matter to me."

Cam bowed slightly and walked away from the podium. The crowd in the auditorium rose to their feet and erupted in raucous applause.

Cam looked humble onstage as he shook Principal Sherman's hand.

Principal Sherman returned to the podium and said, "Thank you, Cam. Everyone, remember to vote tomorrow. The results will be announced right here during our school meeting at ten A.M."

I was so proud of Cam and impressed with how much he had learned.

Behind me, music began. Adventurers crew member Ed was leading the band playing a bouncy tune—Cam's campaign song.

That afternoon, a few minutes before our American Adventurers meeting was set to begin, Cam came bounding into the classroom. Tommy and Freedom were waiting for him, smiling widely.

"Great job, man!" Tommy said. He threw an arm around his shoulder, then lifted Cam's arm in the air like a boxing champion.

Freedom went over and gave Cam a hug. "You did so well, Cam. I am really proud of you." His cheeks turned red with all the attention.

"Was there a speech today?" I joked, clasping my hands

Cam practices his speech before the big day
as Freedom and Tommy look on.

together. "Well done, Cam. Now, grab a seat, guys. This is going to be a fun club meeting today."

As the rest of the students streamed in, I announced, "Good afternoon, everyone. This is an exciting time both here at Manchester Middle School and in our country. There is a student body president vote tomorrow, where you can vote for the candidate who you think will be the best fit for your school. And, in a short time, Americans will vote for the candidate who is best to lead our country." I paused as I looked around the room. "One day, in the not-too-distant future, you too will have that opportunity to vote in the national presidential election. When you do, I hope you will remember some of the things we talked about in these club meetings."

Tommy's hand shot up. "We'll remember our next student body president being dunked in the water, that's for sure!" Everyone started laughing.

"Thanks, man," said Cam, high-fiving Tommy. He had changed out of his jacket and tie and was now wearing a camo-pattern T-shirt.

Just then, Liberty's head popped in the window.

"Hello, Liberty. Glad you could join us," I said.

Liberty shook his body happily as he looked around the classroom. When he spotted Cam he grinned, nodded up and down, and flicked his mane wildly. Freedom laughed and ran over to pat Liberty's nose. He closed his eyes, looking like he was enjoying a day at the spa.

Refocusing the class's attention, I said, "In honor of the elections, Liberty arranged for us to have a special treat today."

"Pizza!" yelled a student from the back of the room.

I laughed. "No, not pizza today, but this is just about as tasty."

The class clapped.

I pulled out a box from under my desk. "These are presidential seals made out of chocolate, graham cracker, and marshmallow. In honor of Cam's campaign, we will call them Cam's Presidential S'mores." I passed one around to each of the students.

"These are cool, Mr. Revere. They look like large chocolate coins. Thank you so much," Freedom said.

"Thank you, too, Liberty!" said a girl sitting next to Tommy.

Liberty seemed to take a bow at the window.

Cam took a bite and said, "This is awesome. Now we have an official name, an official handshake, and an official snack. Our club rocks."

The students laughed as they unwrapped their chocolate wrappers. We played a game called Vote In or Out, where students cast the final votes in a mock election. I printed mock voter registration forms, mock ballots, and we imagined watching the results come in. The time flew by. Before I knew it, the students were leaving the club meeting for the day.

"Remember, we don't have a club meeting tomorrow since the student election voting will be taking place. Don't forget to vote!"

The next morning the students of Manchester Middle School voted in the student body elections. The announcement of the winners was set for the auditorium at 10 A.M. during a school meeting. I arrived a few minutes before the announcement and walked into the auditorium. It appeared to be the whole middle school, just like the day before.

Cam met me at the door. "Good morning, Mr. Revere!" he exclaimed.

"Morning, buddy, how are you feeling about the results?" I asked.

Cam smiled and shrugged his shoulders.

I saw Tommy and Freedom in the middle of a group of students including Ed, happily chatting. Elizabeth was on the other side of the room surrounded by cheerleaders. I stood against a wall, looking around the room.

The time-traveling crew sat as Principal Sherman walked to the podium, carrying an envelope. "We have lots to discuss today, but I wanted to make an announcement regarding the results of the student body elections."

He opened the envelope slowly and pulled out the paper. He squinted looking closely at the envelope, then frowned. Then he smiled and pulled his reading glasses out of his pocket and put them on.

My stomach was in knots.

Principal Sherman continued, "I am sorry about that, everyone. I have trouble reading small print without my glasses. You guys should really print this in a larger font."

He looked over at a teacher, who looked sheepishly back.

"But before I open this envelope, I have a few administrative matters to discuss, beginning with running in class, and lateness . . ." As Principal Sherman spoke about school matters, my mind drifted. I thought of all that Cam had accomplished in the past weeks. We had visited the first three American presidents and first ladies and learned about courage, selflessness, and strategy. Cam studied everything in his playbook, created a team, and inspired the school with his speech.

My mind came back to the auditorium as Principal Sherman

said, "Let's start with the student body president election. Your new president is . . ."

Yesterday, I had suggested that win or lose, Team Cam should meet at our Boston Bagel headquarters today to wrap up the campaign. I did not know how the election would end, but I knew that Cam had grown in the process.

"Your new president is . . ."

I held my breath.

". . . Cameron."

The audience erupted in cheers, and Freedom and Tommy hugged Cam. I let out a long breath and smiled, looking around the room at the happy crowd.

As Principal Sherman continued with the rest of the elected positions, I slipped out the door to find Liberty and share the good news.

Arriving early at Boston Bagels with Liberty, I grabbed a coffee and some bagels, and we found our usual table.

"Mr. President," I said as Cam walked up the sidewalk leading to the bagel shop. Tommy and Freedom walked with him, having all been dropped off by Freedom's grandfather.

"Hi, Mr. Revere and Liberty. Thank you so much for everything you did to help me."

Liberty shook his shoulders. "Congratulations, Cam. Did you tell Elizabeth and the cheerleaders that now they have to get in line to talk with you?"

Cam smiled. "No, she actually shook my hand after I won and said 'Good job.' She didn't look happy, but Principal Sherman looked at her and then she said it. Amazing, I know. Oh, and one of the cheerleaders admitted she took the playbook, and got suspended. She said sorry to me, which was cool. She basically took the blame for Elizabeth, so I said when she's done with the suspension she can help with School Spirit Day. So long as everyone is invited."

Liberty said, "Wow, that is crazy! You are going to be a super president, Cam."

"You really are, Cam," Freedom said sweetly.

"Just don't forget about us now that you are president," said Tommy. "You're still in for throwing the football around later, right?"

Cam nodded and smiled, then opened up his playbook and started writing.

"What are you writing?" Liberty asked, looking puzzled. "I thought the election was over. Why are you still working on your playbook?"

"Oh, I'm looking at all the leadership things I learned from all the presidents and first ladies and Congressman Joseph. Like being courageous, getting a good team, respecting everyone, serving the school, thinking of things bigger than myself. I have lots of work to do now that I am president."

I smiled. "I am very proud of you, Cam. You ran a wonderful race, and you learned the biggest lesson of all—that what you *do* as a president and as a person is more important than how you run your election campaign, or what you *promise to do.*"

Liberty shook his head up and down in agreement and said, "Now, about the special school lunches for horses next year . . .'"

This is the Jefferson Memorial in Washington, D.C. Inside, you
will find passages from the Declaration of Independence.

This is George Washington's second inauguration. Do you recognize other people in this painting?

FROM #1 *NEW YORK TIMES* BESTSELLING AUTHORS

Rush & Kathryn Limbaugh

Visit www.RushRevere.com for more information
on scholarships, quizzes, activities and more!

See your photos at www.Facebook.com/RushRevere

This is Caroline R. of Texas. She and her father,
an Air Force veteran, read a chapter every night before bed.

Don't you just love Mac L. of Virginia's costume? He is dressed as Paul Revere!
He and his sister, Willson, love Liberty and the books!

This is Willa F., who is a student in Florida. Her teacher sent in this wonderful photo of her entry into the Rush Revere Cereal Box Challenge.

Liberty loved playing with the sheepdogs near the Adams family farm.
Do you remember the game they played? This is Abigail, Wellesley,
and Cambridge, the authors' friends.

Acknowledgments

It is hard to believe that this is the fifth book in the Adventures of Rush Revere series. It wasn't long ago that all of this was just an idea in its infancy. Thanks sincerely to you, we now have an extensive Rush Revere family, made up of amazing young patriots, teachers, parents, and grandparents across our great country. It is a true honor to see the heart-melting photos pouring into Liberty's special in-box and read the amazing stories of children thrilled to be visiting the National Archives. We are eternally grateful for your support and inspiration.

As we learned from George Washington and others, it is so important to surround yourself with a dedicated team. Without my team, the Adventures of Rush Revere series simply would not be the same. Thank you from the bottom of my heart to all of you.

My wife, Kathryn, has been the coauthor, visionary, and essential leader behind the entire series since inception. I am extraordinarily proud of Kathryn for her exceptional brilliance, fearless strength, and kind heart. No matter what the challenge or obstacle, she finds a way to overcome or solve it through personal life experience. Kathryn is often the first to start the day in the wee hours of the morning. She leads by tremendous example and cares deeply about connecting with every single reader.

Jonathan Adams Rogers has been our right hand throughout this entire project. His commitment to quality and accuracy is unwavering. Jonathan loves and understands each character in depth. He studies for hours to ensure we include the historic gems and stories that make our country's founding so rare.

I am extremely grateful to have Chris Schoebinger and Christopher Hiers on our team. They are both exceptionally talented and loyal to the success of every single scene and illustration.

A heartfelt thank-you goes out to our parents and families, for teaching us the importance of the free country we live in.

Thank you to the Threshold Editions team for believing in this project, especially Louise Burke, Mitchell Ivers, and Natasha Simons.

Photo Credits

PAGE

ii	Patrick B.
iv	Christopher Hiers
viii	Janice H.
8	Christopher Hiers
21	Christopher Hiers
33	Christopher Hiers
42–43	Getty Images
44	Christopher Hiers
48	dbking
51	Christopher Hiers
55	Christopher Hiers
65	Christopher Hiers
68	The Granger Collection, NYC
80	Wikimedia Commons via the White House Collection/White House Historical Association
81	Yale University Art Gallery
84	Christopher Hiers
90–91	Brooklyn Museum
94	Mellon Collection, National Gallery of Art
95	U.S. Post Office, Bureau of Engraving and Printing
98	Michaele Kayes

100	Washington University Law School, Metropolitan Museum of Art and Crystal Bridges Museum
107	Christopher Hiers
117	Christopher Hiers
121	The Clark Art Institute
127	Wikimedia Commons
131	Christopher Hiers
136	Michaele Kayes
140	Christopher Hiers
142	Getty Images
145	Christopher Hiers
147	Getty Images
150	Christopher Hiers
153	Luke Mathisen
164	Christopher Hiers
171	Christopher Hiers
173	Adams Collection, Massachusetts Historical Society
177	Jonathan Rogers
180	Wikimedia Commons, available at Massachusetts Historical Society
181	Naval Historical Center, U.S. Navy
186–87	Luke Mathisen
188–89	Luke Mathisen
193	John Adams Birthplace, Quincy, Massachusetts, by Daderot is licensed under CC Share Alike 3.0 Unported
194	United States Mint
198–99	Luke Mathisen
208–9	Christopher Hiers
213	Library of Congress
218	The Granger Collection, NYC
220	Wikimedia Commons via the White House Collection/White House Historical Association
222	Christopher Hiers
238	Christopher Hiers
245	Getty Images
247	Library of Congress

248   Luke Mathisen
249   Caroline R.
250   Lauren L.
251   Allison B.
252   Author's Collection
258   Alice T.
259   Stephen P.

These are students from Ms. Alice T.'s class in Florida.
They look just like the Adventurers crew!

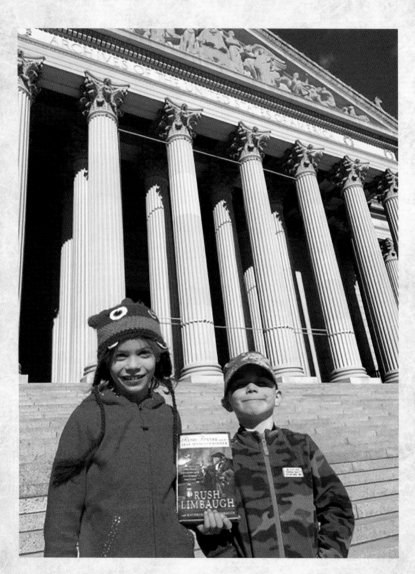

Molly and Patrick P. in front of the National Archives in
Washington, D.C., following "Operation Milkshake."